P M Hubbard was a British writer known principally for his novels of crime and suspense. Born Philip Maitland Hubbard in 1910, he was educated at Elizabeth College in Guernsey and then at Oxford, where he won the Newdigate Prize for English verse in 1933. Serving in the Indian Civil Service from 1934 until its disbandment in 1947, he returned to England to work for the British Council in London. After retiring to work as a freelance writer, he contributed to various publications including *Punch*. Hubbard's first novel, *Flush As May*, was published in 1963, and he went on to publish sixteen more for adults, plus two written for children. The author lived in Dorset and Scotland, and many of his novels draw on his interests and knowledge of country pursuits, small-boat sailing and folk religion. Often set in rural and remote outposts, he viewed place as a central character. In his obituary printed in *The Times* he was described as a 'most imaginative and distinguished practitioner', writing with an 'assurance and individuality of style and tone.' He died in 1980.

THE HOLM OAKS

P M HUBBARD

THE LANGTAIL PRESS
LONDON

This edition published 2011 by
The Langtail Press

www.langtailpress.com

The Holm Oaks © 1965 Caroline Dumonteil, Owain Rhys Phillips and
Maria Marcela Gomez

ISBN 978-1-78002-048-8

THE HOLM OAKS

CHAPTER ONE

I was left the Holt House quite unexpectedly by my Uncle Clarence, who was a bad old uncle I had seen next to nothing of. I never knew why he left it to me. Knowing Uncle Clarence, I think it was probably to hurt someone else, but I never found out who. Whoever they were, they kept their mortification to themselves. If they heard what happened later, it may have been some consolation to them.

When I had the solicitors' letter, I thought of it simply as a superbly convenient legacy. It was convenient because I had just been squeezed out of my job, and I badly needed the money to tide me over until I decided whether to get back into the rat-race or risk working on my own. It was only later that it occurred to me that I now owned two houses and might sell either. The Winchester house would fetch much more than Uncle Clarence's, and must be much more expensive to live in. The Holt House might be habitable. At least it was worth looking at. I went down the next week-end. Elizabeth came with me.

Elizabeth was my wife. She was tall and fair and willowy. When we were first married, she used to look like God's own vestal virgin, which made it all the more impressive when she behaved as she sometimes did. I was crazy about her then, but there is always another side to everything. I suppose it showed how far things had drifted when she went back to her bird-watching, which suited very well her earnest tenacious, rather irritant type of mind. She was in fact very knowledgeable and surprisingly dedicated, and I believe had some quite important scalps under her belt, if that is where you keep scalps. We maintained a reasonably peaceful working surface. I still do not know whether she was as conscious as I was of the depths beneath. There were no children.

It was well into September, and we should really have started the last part of our drive earlier. By the time we came out over the downs and saw the sea it was already almost evening, and the weather did not help. There was heavy cloud everywhere, moving but continuous, and a chilly breeze coming in briskly between grey sea and grey sky. It was not the sort of coast I care for. It was all too gradual. The land just gave up trying and slithered into the sea like an exhausted swimmer. There were no rocks, no cliffs, only an endless shingle beach, carved out in places where a stream ran out or the sea had broken in and turned itself into an only half-salt lagoon. Even from where we were you could hear the sea on the beach. The whole south was full of it. It would be hell when the wind blew. The area had been scheduled by the planners as one of great natural beauty, but that must have been when the sun was out. It had a fascination, but I did not warm to it. We got back into the car and drove down into Marlock.

Marlock undoubtedly looked like a village in a scheduled area. It was stone and thatch. The street wound picturesquely and the woodwork was well painted. There was a post office that sold a lot of other things, a shop where you could buy stamps and a pub called the Anchor. When I asked for the Holt House, the post-mistress turned her eyes up, as if the previous owner had left a bill unpaid or ruined her daughter. From what I remembered of Uncle Clarence, he might well have done either, though in the natural course of things the first seemed more likely. He must have been all of eighty when he died.

We drove on seawards, with the land falling away on both sides of us. The road was still tarmac, but only just. Then it turned right-handed over a narrow bridge, and as the car bounced over it two great birds got up heavily from a steel sheet of water on our right.

Elizabeth said, 'Stop, Jake, for God's sake,' and flung herself out of the near-side door with her glasses at the ready. For three or four seconds she stood there by the palpitating car, bent forward and following the circling birds with the glasses. If she had had a tail, it would have stuck straight out behind and twitched slightly. Then she lowered the glasses and let herself back into the car. She was a little breathless. 'Pink-foots,' she said. 'Jake, they're pink-foots.' I resigned myself from that moment to living at the Holt House, which I had never yet seen. I could not in the nature of things know what it could do to us all, but there seemed in any case to be no alternative.

A minute later I saw a house to the left of the road straight ahead. It was silhouetted against the sky, and must have been right over the beach. It was brick and looked hideous. At the same moment the holm oaks came up on our right. There seemed to be five or six acres of them in a long strip, clinging to the last slope of land above the shingle. I was as much a maniac for trees, in my way, as Elizabeth was for birds, but these were interesting rather than beautiful. They were very close-grown, and none of them more than twenty or thirty feet high. Elizabeth pointed to my side of the road. 'There,' she said.

There was an iron farm-gate in the right-hand fence and a board said 'The Holt House'. For a moment I was confused and then relieved. The brick house, at least, was not for us. For us a track led off, rubble-paved but motorable, skirting the landward side of the wood. I got out and opened the gate.

We jolted along for nearly a quarter of a mile, almost under the edge of the brooding trees. They were built to stand the southwest gales, and here on the lee side the breeze did not move them at all. They were quite silent and even muffled the voice of the sea. It was dark already inside the wood, but I could see the scarlet seed-pods of stinking iris glowing like coral on the black leaf-mould. I suppose this was the holt. At any rate, when we turned round the far end of the wood, there was the Holt House, right in front of us.

It was all of cream-coloured stone, very straight up and down and uncompromising. There were tall sash-windows on the ground and first floors and the dormers of a second floor broke the slope of the roof. It was not a big house. There was something a little forbidding in the way it stood up out of that flat, shelving landscape, but it did not lack character. It was National Trust stuff compared with that red-brick horror at the other end of the wood. What with this and the pink-footed geese, I began to think better of my Uncle Clarence than I had yet.

There was no made garden, but close-cut grass between stone walls all round the house. Behind, the flat green stretched away westwards along the coast as far as one could see. On the landward side there was a single paddock between the house and the lagoon where we had put up the geese. On the seaward side there was nothing but a short green slope to the edge of the shingle. In front, eastwards, the edge of the oak wood ran within twenty yards of the front gate. The wood was unfenced, and I saw there was a path leading from the gate straight into it. This would give direct access to the metalled road, but only for people on foot. Anything on wheels had to go, as we had come, round the north side of the trees.

We had not told anyone we were coming. We did not expect to find the house open, and it was not. We walked round it, talking in half-whispers against the perpetual mutter of the sea, and flattened our noses on the ground-floor windows. There was no furniture and the windows were uncurtained. Whatever possessions Uncle Clarence had had, they had gone elsewhere. The house, stripped, silent and empty, was ours and there to receive us. It was not a shiny house, but there was nothing visibly wrong with it. So far as appearances went, we could move in tomorrow. I did not know quite what went with it, but the wood at least should be ours.

I walked back to the gate and looked up at the front of the house. I could still find nothing against it. It was unforthcoming but strictly neutral. The place was different. It would take a lot of living in.

Outside the gate, where the rubble road ended, there were two paths, one going straight ahead into the wood and one right-handed towards the beach. I turned right-handed and a moment later heard Elizabeth pattering after me. She said, 'Jake, Jake, wait for me. It's lovely, don't you think?'

'It's not lovely,' I said. 'That's the geese. It could be ghastly. I admit it could be superb at times. It's a hell of an undertaking. What do you think Stella would make of it?'

Stella was Elizabeth's younger sister, and the only other more or less permanent member of the household. Elizabeth said, 'Stella?' I knew the tone at once. It meant, roughly speaking, that so far as she was concerned Stella could do what she liked about it, and it was up to me to feel the same. 'I think Stella would approve,' she said. 'There's lots to paint.'

I came out on to the top of the beach and saw, stretching away straight on both sides of me, the vast sweep of banked pebbles, with the sea lying level in front of it and the grey downs raising themselves reluctantly behind. Stella was a sad person, and her art, though she made a sort of living at it, always seemed to me a sad art. She might like the place, in fact. And she need not be here all the time, which was more than could be said for me. I said, 'Yes, I suppose she might. Who do you think lives in that brick abortion over on the road? They'd be our only neighbours, by the look of it. Not but that the wood is a pretty effective insulator.'

'Farmer, probably. All the land is in hand, and we're some way from the village.'

We picked our way eastwards along the top of the shingle, where the dense-packed stones never shifted, and the coarse green of the land's edge found its way up between them. When we came to the corner of the wood, I stopped. I peered in under the trees but did not want to go into them. It was grey dusk now out on the beach and the wood was quite dark. Even from here the trees made no sound that could make itself heard above the noise of the sea. Only holm oaks could have made a wood of this size in a place like this, and they did not really like it. They had turned their backs on the sea, and their packed tops had built themselves into a long wind-repellent curve as the land climbed under them.

Somewhere behind me Elizabeth gave a yelp, and I turned and went back to her. She was standing a little way down the slope of the beach, looking down at a dead bird spread-eagled on the pebbles. It had been dead some time, but it had been shot. 'Cormorant,' I said. 'They're vermin, you know.'

She shook her head. 'They oughtn't to shoot them,' she said.

'The sea's big enough, and they're lovely birds.'

'Tell that to the fishermen,' I said. I walked on, saw, at two different places, orange cartridge cases between the grey stones and then stopped dead. I did not share my wife's addiction, but even I did not think anyone ought to shoot terns. I hoped Elizabeth would not see it, but she was close behind me and before I could alter course, she caught my arm.

'Jake,' she said. 'Jake, it's horrible. Who could do a thing like that?'

'Boys, probably. Anyone can have a shotgun, and anything flying is fair game if you're ignorant enough.'

'I won't have it here.' She spoke thickly, through almost shut teeth. I knew that voice.

I said, 'You won't?' I stopped and looked at her, and for a second or two we stood and faced each other. She was almost as tall as I was, and her face was only just below mine. Her eyes opened wide and stared into my eyes. It had been a great trick of hers in the old days. Her eyes were very long and blue. She said, 'Jake, we are coming here, aren't we? We must. I love it here.'

I had not really anything to say. After all, the house was mine. There was no stake money. I could sell it as well in six months' time as I could now. And I did not know anything decisive against it. If the balance of advantage was adverse, time would bring it to account. I was conscious, in some way, of the venture, which poor Elizabeth was not, but I could not reject it out of hand.

'All right,' I said. 'But we must come and have a proper look at it. It's no good hanging about now. It will be pitch dark in half an hour.'

We walked back along the beach to the corner of the wood. As we turned up the path, something in the trees choked horribly. It was not an easy sound to describe, but in that dark, unpopulated place, it was extraordinarily unpleasant. I said, 'What the hell's that?'

We stood and listened, but nothing happened. I had not the least wish to go and investigate. 'Come on,' I said. I made for the car, and Elizabeth, a moment later, came after me. A bird came out of the wood, hardly visible against the dark cloudbank, and flew heavily across in the direction of the lagoon. It was a biggish bird, as big as a crow; only no decent crow would be out at that time of night. I stopped by the car. 'See him?' I said. 'What was he? Heavy sort of flyer.'

Elizabeth stood there, staring after the long invisible bird. Then she shook her head. 'I – I don't know,' she said. She seemed a little breathless. 'I've never seen anything—' She stopped and got into the car. 'We'll see him again,' she said.

I drove cautiously back along the top edge of the wood and got out to open the gate. Even if it was my gate, it had not seemed right to leave it open. I ran the car out on to the road and stopped. There were lights showing down to the right. 'Let's go and have a look at the neighbours,' I said.

'You're not going to talk to them?'

'No, I don't think so. Just have a look at them. It's dark enough and they've got plenty of lights on.'

I ran down the road quietly with only the sidelights burning. This house had a garden. Even in the near-darkness, it looked prim and almost suburban. Whatever it was, it was no farm. The house was a brick box with a high-pitched roof and fancy features, and there was a garage and a couple of small outhouses. There were no farm-buildings. However and whenever it had got here, it might just as well have been in Wimbledon. There was an ornamental wrought-iron gate incorporating what was presumably the name of the house. It was called Holm Oaks. I stopped the car. We both got out and stood there in the dark narrow road, staring incredulously at this unexpected addition to the local amenities.

The windows of the ground-floor front were brightly lit and uncurtained, but the house was a bit above the level of the road, and our private view began only halfway up the walls. As we watched, a woman's head moved across the room. All I could see was that it was a dark head. I did not think she could be very tall, but it was difficult to judge. There was a sudden flurry of music, and a tenor voice rang out with enormous clarity, '*Nessun dorma*—'

It was canned music, of course. One of the pop operatic singers, by the sound of him. Not my sort of music, in fact, but coming out of that brick villa in that sea-shot wilderness it was startlingly beautiful.

'Mm,' said Elizabeth. 'Cultural types. Hundred favourite classics.'

For no very good reason, I rallied to the defence of Holm Oaks. 'Some people like it,' I said. 'It's a marvellous voice.'

Elizabeth said, 'Well—' Then the front door opened, and a very tall man came down a couple of steps into the front garden. We ducked, simultaneously and instinctively, like guilty children. I was thankful I had left the car a bit up the road. The whole situation was completely ridiculous, and I had a strong inclination to giggle. I think if he had walked down to the gate and seen us, I could not have gone to live in the Holt House at all, and the whole of what followed would never have happened. But he stood there, at the top of the sloping garden, with the brightly lit hall behind him, and none of us moved. Only the beautiful tenor voice sang on in self-conscious ecstasy.

I never saw exactly what happened. There was a sharp snap, as if something had been broken suddenly in mid-air. I heard the man move, and when I looked again, he had turned and was facing back into the doorway. The singer paused, and against a rather muted orchestra I heard a woman's voice call, 'Dennis! Have you found it?'

The man said, 'No, I don't know where it is.' He threw something, quite deliberately, into the darkness beside him. Then he went inside and shut the door. The singer started up again, but was cut off short in the middle of a lovely high note.

I said, 'Come on,' and we straightened up and scuttled back to the car.

CHAPTER TWO

Elizabeth went down to Marlock three days later to see the drains and the heating, and saw two Bean geese, and a rare sort of sea-bird whose proper name I forget. I know that when I called it a Queen Tern, she said it was unworthy of me, as perhaps it was. I wrote to my Uncle Clarence's executors and said that I had decided to take personal possession of the Holt House and occupy it myself, at least temporarily. I asked them for details of the land that went with the house. They had said it was five acres more or less, and I asked them particularly to confirm that this included the wood.

I do not know whether Elizabeth or I was more shocked by their reply. They said that the land going with the house lay mainly to the west of it and embraced three sides of Marlock Mere, which I took to be the lagoon where Elizabeth had seen the pink-foots. The wood had formerly been part of the property, but the late Mr Haddon had sold it shortly before his death to a Mr Wainwright, who was understood to be a resident of the locality.

I do not think we either of us for a moment doubted who Mr Wainwright was or where he lived. Unless we were all at sea, Mr Wainwright was called Dennis and lived in a house already called Holm Oaks. All he had done was to make his actual property measure up to its fancy name. What Uncle Clarence had been at, unless it was the sheer irresponsibility of the moribund elderly, we could not imagine. For the matter of that, his decision to leave the house to me might have been equally outrageous, but I do not think I could be expected to see it like that.

At any rate, there we were. If we moved into the Holt House, our nearest neighbour would not, as we had thought, be a quarter of a mile away, but, if he chose, a matter of twenty yards from our gate. The enormously tall Mr Wainwright, who snapped things in his hands outside his front door at night, and then went inside to turn off his wife's wireless, could if he wanted lurk in the trees and watch us, as we, from the most innocent motives, had watched him. What his reasons might be for doing anything of the sort I could not imagine. But I did not like the possibility, and Elizabeth certainly did not like being deprived of her expected rights in the wood, which she was by now pretty certain contained something specially exotic in the way of birds. We both felt that we had been in some way cheated of our inheritance, though it was probably only myself who saw how unreasonable the feeling was.

'There must be a right of way,' I said. 'There's that path through the wood from the gate. It's the only direct access to the road. However wicked or potty Uncle Clarence was, his solicitors wouldn't have let him part with his right-of-way through. And in that case you've got the run of the wood in practice, unless Dennis fences the path. And I really can't see why in the world he should. At any rate, you've got three sides of the Mere, which is where the geese are. I can't say I'm all that keen on the wood myself. I'm glad it's there, of course, but I'm not dead set on spending much time in it. Do you remember what stinking iris smells like?'

Elizabeth shook her head. She was not really listening. 'At least as bad as it sounds,' I said. 'Carrion, more or less. It's difficult to believe that a healthy vegetable can smell so like dead animal.'

She shook her head again. 'I've got an idea about that wood,' she said. 'It may be all nonsense, but it could be tremendous. It's only a matter of watching.'

'And it doesn't worry you that, if you do find a colony of Great Auks there, they're Dennis's Auks, not yours?'

'Of course it worries me. I hope your Uncle Clarence is roasting in hell fire for doing this to us. But I've still got to go and see if the Great Auks are there.'

Stella was told about Marlock that evening. She spent a lot of time in London, and used the room she kept with us only when she felt like it. I was in the sitting-room when I heard Elizabeth say, 'Oh hullo, Stella. You know this house Jake's been left at Marlock? We're going to sell this and go and live there.'

Stella came into the room first with Elizabeth behind her. She was five years younger and a head shorter. She was as slight as her sister, but the slightness had a bony quality, even at sight, which you never noticed in Elizabeth, at least until you came to grips with her. Also, she was as dark as Elizabeth was fair. They were different in every sort of way.

Stella said, 'Hullo, Jake. Pretty rushed decision, isn't it?'

'Only the Marlock side. There's nothing to keep me here in any case. Now there's this house sitting there empty, all ours if we want it. It seems a pity not to try it. If it doesn't do, I can always sell it and look for something else.'

Elizabeth said, 'But—' She stood there, looking from one to the other of us.

Stella turned to her. 'But what?' she said. 'It seems a reasonable view.'

'I shan't want to sell it. I think it's lovely.'

For a moment Stella considered her. Then she turned to me. 'Tell me about it,' she said.

'It's pretty fantastic. The sort of place you've got to come to terms with if you can. There's an endless shingle beach on one side, miles of it, and a sort of salt lagoon on the other. Marlock Mere, apparently. And a wood of holm oaks in front, almost on top of the beach.'

'Which we don't own,' said Elizabeth. She went out of the room, shutting the door behind her.

'We don't own it,' I said, 'because my blighted uncle sold it to the neighbours just before he died.'

'There are neighbours?'

'At the other end of the wood, a quarter of a mile away. Unknown quantity in a red-brick villa.'

Stella sat down and looked at me. 'What do you really think, Jake?' she said.

'I really think it's worth trying. I think you might like it, as a matter of fact. It's a nice house.'

'But a doubtful place?'

'Doubtful, yes. It could go either way.'

She nodded. 'Birds, I imagine?'

'Plenty of birds. Geese and all sorts. Only somebody seems to be shooting them a bit.'

'The neighbour?'

'I don't know. I hope not, for everyone's sake.'

She nodded again. 'You're the boss,' she said. 'When do we move?'

'Pretty soon, I imagine. We'd want to be well dug in before it starts to blow us off the beach.'

'Right. It's a long way from London, but I think I'm rather looking forward to it.'

'I hope to God you're right,' I said.

I myself saw the inside of the Holt House for the first time during the last few days of September, and we moved in bag and baggage at the end of the first week in October. In point of fact there was as little wrong with it inside as there was out. Uncle Clarence had made himself comfortable in his wilderness, and even if the household machinery was not architect-designed or up to the minute, it all worked. Elizabeth, who had got what she very badly wanted, but knew she was dragging me behind her, went about in a curious kind of determined happiness. I took advantage of the moral climate to leave most of the work to her. She nobbled for herself the first-floor room looking towards the mere. This did not worry me – I preferred sea and trees – but it was the only room with a north light. Stella could have the run of the second floor, but the dormers were all east or west, and, as usual, not very big. Stella did not move with us. She said she would come down later when the worst was over. I think privately she preferred to make the best of the pickings rather than risk a clash with Elizabeth over the main carcass. I had all the ordinary man's horror of the rows that occasionally blew up between them. Stella knew this perfectly well, and for the most part, where there was war, she kept it cold.

Early on the second afternoon I left Elizabeth to it and walked out of the gate and into Mr Wainwright's wood. As I had thought, the path went straight through to the road, and our right-of-way had been preserved. The thing was a plantation, not natural woodland. Someone had put it down, I suppose, three generations back, and had seen the trees well up before they had let go their hold. Since then nothing much had been done. There had been no thinning, and with few early failures the trees were now much too close together. Also they had been allowed to branch too low, and the whole wood had heeled over slightly in the prevailing south-westerly winds. There was an impenetrable tangle not very far above one's head and there could be next to no daylight, even in summer. The path itself was clear, but the rides leading off it were blocked with debris and bleached undergrowth. It was a sad place, even at that time of day and in still weather. The sound of the sea on the beach, which varied in intensity but never stopped, was no more than a whisper. There was no other sound whatever. If there were birds in the wood, they were very silent ones.

There was a lot, even now, I could do with that wood, but it was not mine to do anything with. All I could do was walk through it, and this I did, over the spongy green of the path, until I saw daylight at the far end, with the tarmac of the road gleaming at the bottom of the gap. There were no fences or stiles. As I got closer to the end, the far side of the road took on a familiar look, and I saw it was the Wainwrights' garden hedge. The path came out almost, but not exactly, opposite the house.

I paused, approached the gap cautiously, put my head out into the road and found Mr Wainwright leaning on his ornamental front gate. His head turned my way at the same moment, and for a time we looked at each other, steadily if slightly askew, across the width of the road. Then he straightened up and I stepped out on to the tarmac. We both managed a smile at about the same moment. I only hoped my eyes were a bit less obviously watchful than his were. His smile hardly got above the bottom of his nose. He was a very tall, stiff man, and curiously neat. In a place and weather which sent me naturally to superimposed jerseys he wore a solid dark suit with a collar and tie. I wondered whether he had been somebody's butler, but he did not sound like it. He said, 'You'll be Mr Haddon. I heard you'd moved in.' There was a faintly Celtic flavour somewhere, but it was the voice he had grown up with and argued an educated background.

'That's right,' I said. 'Mr Wainwright?'

He nodded. He had forgotten to keep his smile going, and was looking down at me with undisguised appraisal. He stood the height of a stone step above me, and was in any case at least half a head taller. I reached the outside of the gate and stood there, still without saying anything. It was his turn to do the talking.

He suddenly smiled again, much more successfully this time. 'Well, come in,' he said. He opened the gate and stood aside. If he had actually said, 'Will you walk into my parlour?', I could hardly have agreed more reluctantly. There was nothing I could put my finger on, but I was very glad the wood was as long and thick as it was.

The garden was as neat as he was, and the house did not improve with full daylight. It would not have mattered if it had been in Wimbledon, but it was very uncomfortable where it was. And there was nothing suburban about the man himself. His head was more like a don's than a stockbroker's, with bony frontal lobes, deep-set grey eyes and hollow cheeks; only no don I ever saw dressed like that.

He showed me into the room on the right, which was the room we had seen the top half of from over the garden hedge. There was a big radiogram in the corner which accounted for the operatic tenor. He said, 'Sit down, Mr Haddon.' He sat opposite me and put his hands on his knees. He was still smiling as if he shared some joke with me and expected me to know what it was.

Presently he took the plunge. 'The Mr Haddon we knew was your uncle?' he said.

'Yes, that's right.' I was not going to help him out, and in any case the less said about Uncle Clarence the better.

He thought about this. Then he said, 'This is a very lonely part of the country.'

'Yes?' I said. 'Yes, I can imagine it might be.'

'Of course,' he said, 'I don't know what your interests are.'

I hesitated between necromancy and numismatics. Finally I said, 'I've just left a job in Winchester.'

'Ah,' he said, as if this told him everything he had hoped for. 'You have yet to find your interests here, perhaps.'

'Perhaps so, yes. Of course,' I said, feeling as if I was conceding a pawn, 'a new place is always interesting in itself.'

'Oh yes, indeed.' He looked out of the window for a moment. It was the first time he had taken his eyes off me. He said, 'We have been here nearly five years now.' He switched his eyes back to mine again, as if anxious not to miss my reaction to this. I tried to think what my reaction ought to be, but could come to no sort of conclusion at all. I was conscious of a steady weakening of my position, as if I was being forced back into a corner. I side-stepped instinctively. 'We were in our last house six years,' I said. I was back in the centre of the ring, and decided to carry the fight to him.

I said, 'Do you farm any land, Mr Wainwright?'

He must have known the answer to this at least as well as I did, and I knew it for certain. I have never seen anything less like a farmer. Nevertheless, he thought all round the question before committing himself. I watched him with polite interest, and in the back of my mind tried to imagine what the Wainwright family's conversation would be like over the breakfast table. I was wondering what happened if Mrs Wainwright offered him a choice between poached and scrambled, when he said, 'Well, no. No, I've never done any farming. There's the garden, of course.'

'Of course. I'm not much of a gardener myself, I'm afraid.' Strengthened by this confession, I gathered my feet under me and started to get up. Then the door opened and Mrs Wainwright came in.

The only two things I had so far any reason to suspect about her were that she was small and dark haired. Both were correct. She was very small in every direction, but so completely in harmony with herself that her smallness did not strike me until I actually stood up and found myself looking down at her. One did not think of her as a little woman. She was beautifully shaped, but there was nothing cosy or kittenish about her. Nor did she look in the least like a china doll, a Dresden shepherdess or any other sort of earthenware. There was no suggestion of brittleness, either in her appearance or in her voice. She was smooth, shiny and self-contained, a lot younger than her husband and twice as sure of herself. All these things are a matter of taste, but to me Mrs Wainwright was, instantaneously and inevitably, pure dynamite.

Mr Wainwright heaved himself to his feet and said, 'You haven't met my wife, perhaps?', as if even that was something he was not entirely sure about.

'No,' I said. I stood there looking at Mrs Wainwright in what I felt certain was a rather inappropriate manner, and she stood looking at me with friendly but completely dispassionate appraisal.

'This is Mr Haddon,' he said. 'He has just moved in to the Holt House. With his family, I think? I believe you have a family, Mr. Haddon?'

Mrs Wainwright's hand was silk-smooth, firm and quite cold. We made the appropriate murmurs, and I managed to get my eyes off her and back to her husband. 'At the moment,' I said, 'only my wife. My sister-in-law will be joining us occasionally.' I went on with my drift towards the door. I did not at all like being there with the two of them together. I said I must be going, it was time I went back to help my wife with the unpacking, she would be wondering what had happened to me.

Neither of them said anything at all. We all drifted out through the front door into the neat front garden and down as far as the gate. I said I was glad we had met; we should be meeting again, no doubt. This took me out of the gate and on to the road. Mrs Wainwright stood just inside the gate and her husband behind her. The difference in height was almost grotesque. She said, 'Did you come by the wood, Mr Haddon?'

I said, 'Yes,' and she nodded. I got myself across the road and into the opening of the path. I suppose I must have said good-bye. I am fairly sure neither of them did.

I went through the wood slowly, staring at the green moss as I trod on it. I had the answer to one at least of Mr Wainwright's questions. I had found one thing to interest me here for a start.

CHAPTER THREE

As soon as we were at all settled, the cloud blew off and the wind dropped, and we went into a week of St Luke's summer. The sunlight lay flat and yellow all day to the cloudless horizons, and the sea whispered on the beach as peacefully as a municipal reservoir in a drowned Welsh valley. Only the oak-wood remained impervious to the enchantment. The trees had seen too much weather to trust any of it, and bowed themselves resolutely over their private darkness. Elizabeth lay out most of the day with her glasses and her notebooks in a hide she had built herself overlooking the mere, and at other times, especially in the evening, went walking in the wood looking for something she did not find. I also walked in the wood, but at other times and looking, I suppose, for something quite different. Like her, I did not find what I was looking for, or not then.

What I did find was that if I turned off the path fifty yards or so before it reached the road and made my way parallel with the path and a bit to the north of it, I could come to the edge of the trees right opposite the red-brick house. I made myself, with time, a devious but reasonably clear passage there, and used to stand, satisfactorily screened, but with the whole front of the house visible to me, waiting for a glimpse of the quiet, white woman who, it seemed to me, so incongruously lived there. I had not behaved like this since I was about sixteen, but I could not, even under severe self-examination, be brought to admit that there was anything undignified in it. Carol Wainwright was no Lolita, nor even a little tobacconist's blonde. She was what I had been looking for, consciously or unconsciously, ever since I had lost my illusions about Elizabeth. Even at this stage, when we had hardly more than seen each other, I had no doubts about this.

Oddly enough, it was I who finally found what Elizabeth was looking for. I suppose I should be thankful that it was not the other way round. I went into the wood after tea, in the last red light of a perfect evening. I walked, automatically and without any real hope or purpose, to my hide opposite the Wainwrights' house, and as I got there the lights went on in a first-floor window, and Carol Wainwright came and stood just inside the window, with the lights behind her and the last of the daylight on her face. For half a minute or more she stood there, looking out over the wood to the fading saffron sky westwards. It was impossible to see what her expression was. Then she made a small gesture of resignation and, crossing her hands over in the way women do, pulled her jersey over her head. There was nothing in the least improper in this. I had a glimpse of very smooth arms and shoulders, but no more than I could have seen if she had been wearing a dinner-frock and much less than if she had been wearing a bathing-dress. It was the loneliness and casual intimacy of the gesture that hit me between wind and water. I had the feeling that I had been, for a second or two, alone in her room with a woman who had seemed to carry an almost tangible privacy about with her.

She did not come back to the window; and in any case if she had proceeded to strip herself naked in full view, I should not have stayed to see. I mention this, not to falsify, as it well might, my general picture of myself, but to show the sort of state I had already got into over Carol Wainwright. I hope I do not wrong the generality of my sex when I say that the man who would turn his back on a piece of unsolicited voyeurism is, unless he happens to be a saint, at least a bit of a case.

It was almost completely dark in the wood now. I went back slowly, but more from an unreasonable wish to prolong my walk than because I could not see my way. I was getting to know the wood very well, and was conscious of an increasing respect for it. If you feel about trees as I do, individual trees, even in a wood as homogeneous and close-grown as this, soon assume personal characteristics, and you steer from known tree to known tree through the crowd of still undifferentiated others. So I went slowly but without hesitation, touching the familiar stems as I passed them. My mind was almost entirely taken up with what I had just seen, but I liked the wood better because of it.

I was almost at the far edge, and beginning to see a glimmer of vestigial daylight between the trees in front, when something flopped down out of the darkness above me and took off in a heavily dipped course just over my head. I thought at first it was an owl, but an owl that flew as badly as that would never catch anything. Also there was a double streak of white at the back of it as it went ahead of me. It looked like a barrister who had put his bands on back to front and was finding it difficult to fly in his gown. It was not like any sort of owl I had ever seen. I lost it before it was clear of the trees, and of course it was gone by the time I was clear of them myself. It had flapped off somewhere into the dusk, but what it was doing at this time of night, or what it had been up to in the wood, I had no idea.

I met Elizabeth coming out of the gate. She was hurrying as if she was late for an important appointment. She said, 'Have you just come from the wood?'

'Yes.' I wondered whether any explanation was needed, but at this stage I did not think it was. The time for explanations came later. At this stage I was alone with a purely private experience.

She said, 'Did you see anything?'

I had a lunatic impulse to say, 'Yes, thank you, I was just in time,' but of course I did not say it. Instead I said, 'A bird flew out of the trees just ahead of me. Heavy sort of chap. I didn't see where he went.'

She said, 'Could it be the one we saw the other evening?'

'Which other evening?'

'The first time we came down. It flew out of the wood, do you remember, as we came back to the car. It went off towards the mere.'

'I remember, yes. It could be the same. I didn't see much of him that time. This was a funny one, all right.'

'Funny how?' She was almost breathless in her anxiety.

'Well, as I said – an ungainly flyer. Oh, and he had a white streak on him somewhere, at the back, I think.'

'Jake—' Elizabeth clutched me by the arms and looked up at me with the sort of expression on her face she had once used for very different reasons and with a very different effect. 'Jake, do you mean here? A pair of white streaks here?' She took one hand off me and traced the line of an imaginary pigtail down the back of her slender neck.

I thought. 'It could be,' I said. 'He was flying away from me, and it was almost dark. But what I saw could have been something like that. Is it important?'

Elizabeth let go of me and turned to look over in the direction of the mere. She said almost under her breath, 'The nuchal plumes. The nuchal plumes, by golly.' She turned back to me. 'He didn't say anything?' she asked.

'Not a word. Should he have? He almost fell on my neck. I suppose he might have apologised, but I think in his ungainly sort of way he was in a hurry. Now tell me what I have missed.'

She shook her head. 'You haven't missed anything,' she said. 'I have, apparently. But I'll see him again. It seems almost too good to be true but I think – I think it might be a Night Heron. It was that cry that first gave me the idea. Do you remember that evening, in the wood, as we came up from the beach?'

I remembered it now. 'Horrible choking noise?' I said. 'I thought something was being throttled. I didn't like it a bit.'

'That's it. That's it, don't you see? Like a man vomiting, the book says.'

'It was all of that.'

'That and the two white plumes at the back of the neck. And a heavy slow flyer, about the size of a crow. Jake, it really is a heron, I believe.' She took a long breath. '*Nycticorax*,' she said.

'You can say that again,' I said.

'I can,' she said. She laughed rapturously. '*Nycticorax nycticorax*. That's its proper name. *Nycticorax nycticorax*, according to Linnaeus. Jake, it's fabulous.'

'And now you'll be in all the books?' I said.

I had not meant to say it indulgently. I still wanted Elizabeth to be happy, and I was pleased to see her so elated, but she turned on me rather fiercely. 'Oh, don't be silly,' she said. 'I haven't discovered the damned bird. But it's a very rare visitor, and an observation is important. Only I must get a cast-iron identification. And I don't think they ever stay much later than this. I wish I could see it by day, but they roost, you see, in the woods all day, and only come out at night to feed. I expect this one feeds down by the mere.'

I said, 'If he makes that obscene noise anywhere down by the mere at night, you ought to be able to catch up with him. You'll never find him in the wood if he chooses to lie up there all day. With that colouring and the trees as thick as they are you couldn't see him in a hundred years.' It was perfectly true, but I was conscious, even while I said it, that for some possible future reason I did not want Elizabeth wandering about in the wood all day. The evenings would have to take their chance. It was very dark in the wood in the evenings, and there was plenty of room for people to be there without seeing each other. And in any case, in the evenings *Nycticorax* would be out on the mere, vomiting happily to himself and poking about for whatever nasty sort of food he fancied. The holm oak was never my favourite tree, but by God, I thought, your Night Heron was not the most elegant of birds. For the moment, at any rate, the wood was no good to Elizabeth. She turned, and we went into the house together.

She said, 'What about these Wainwrights? Ought I to go and see them? They don't sound very gay, from all you say.'

I had seen this coming. 'They're not,' I said. 'She's quite pleasant, but doesn't say much, and he's a decided oddity. I don't see why you need make any point of seeing them. We're bound to run into them one way or another soon. But it's up to you. You may get a bigger hand from them than I got. So far as I'm concerned, I don't know anything against them yet, but I'd even rather they owned the wood than that it wasn't there at all. They don't seem to do much with it, I must say. I wonder what he wanted it for and how much he paid for it?'

Elizabeth was up in arms at once. 'They wouldn't do anything to it, would they?'

'I hope to God not. I am getting to like it more and more. Only it could do with a bit of proper attention. I wonder if old Wainwright would sell it back to me? But I'd better find out first what he gave for it.'

'Do you really think he'd sell?'

'It's no good – I simply don't know what he'd do in any circumstances. If you can make any more of him than I can, you're welcome to try. But I'll tell you one thing. I may be wronging him, but I have a strong suspicion that nothing would make him so hell-bent on anything as the feeling that we were against it.'

'Us in particular?'

'I don't know about that. He may be like that with everybody. But us, certainly. It's only my guess, of course. But I fancy if you told our Dennis that *nycticorax* favoured a particular tree, you'd find that that was just the tree that had been marked out for thinning. If you want *nycti* back next year, the best thing you can do is to beg Dennis to cut down the lot.'

'You make him sound a poppet, I must say. But don't worry. I'm not putting any ideas in his head.' She got up and went to the door. 'Stella phoned,' she said. 'Did I tell you? She's coming down this evening.'

'Oh? No. Good.'

Elizabeth knew that she had not told me, and knew that I knew this. It was a sort of game to be played on established lines and according to certain rules. Elizabeth had to display a complete indifference to her sister's feelings, movements and general well-being, and I was expected to reflect this attitude. I did not keep it up with Stella herself, of course. I talked straight to her, straighter, perhaps than I ever talked to anyone. I liked her company, and was glad when she chose to join the household, which she would now, I imagined, do less frequently and for fewer days at a time. This also, I do not doubt, Elizabeth knew, but so long as it was not allowed to appear too openly, she did not seem to mind, or at least was prepared to accept it. I believed that if Stella was ever in any real trouble, Elizabeth might worry over her and do her best for her. But Stella had long been established as the capable one of the family. Nothing ever did go wrong with Stella. She lived her own life and managed her own affairs without, so far, a husband to help her out. Elizabeth, as the elder sister and mistress of a household Stella chose to frequent, answered this independence with a sort of studied casualness in respect of everything she did. I had not up to then found any particular difficulty in playing third man to this odd relationship, but this was mostly because no one was ever ready to push the thing to a point where the seams began to open up. There were, so far as I knew, no great depths of emotion involved, and one or the other of the parties was always ready to sheer off if a direct clash seemed imminent.

So I said, 'Oh? No. Good,' and took up my crossword as if my train of thought had scarcely been disturbed. Perhaps, in fact, it had not. My mental preoccupation with a woman I had barely been introduced to was already beginning to insulate me considerably in my other relations. But it would be nice to have Stella down and see what she made of the place.

I heard her car about an hour later and went down to the gate to meet her. Elizabeth was out. She had probably gone down to the mere after *nycticorax*. Stella climbed out of the car and stood up stretching her legs. She said, 'Hullo, Jake.' Then she walked, not up to the house, but straight down the path to the beach, and stood there, on the top ridge of the shingle, looking about her. It was quite dark now, but the sky was as clear as it had been all day and the stars were brilliant. The winter stars were starting to show up at nights, and I thought I could see the Pleiades heaving themselves coyly out of the mists in the south-east. The sea, luminous in itself and barely wrinkled, kept up its Mediterranean whisper all along the beach.

'Golly,' said Stella. It was a family word. She and Elizabeth both used it. She turned and came back up the path and we went in through the gate and up to the house. In the lighted hall, she threw off her head-scarf and loosened the collar of her coat. Her bony, intense face emerged suddenly from a sort of cloak of impersonality, and she looked at me sideways.

'What a place, Jake,' she said. 'Do you realise what you've let yourself in for?'

I nodded. 'I think so. It's a bit all or nothing, isn't it?'

'That's a mild way of putting it. So long as you know what you're doing.'

'I haven't committed myself,' I said. 'I can always sell it if I want to.'

She smiled. 'Don't kid yourself,' she said. 'If you're here six months, you'll never get away.'

'I'll risk it.'

'Where's Elizabeth?'

'Down by the mere, I think. You passed it when you came over the bridge. There's some fabulous night-bird reared its remarkably ugly head, and she's out looking for it.'

'Show me the house, then.'

'I'm on the south-east corner,' I said as we went upstairs. 'Elizabeth has got the north room, so that she can keep an eye on the mere. There's a nice south-west room you could have, or you can take your pick of the second floor. I've put your things up there for the time, but it's for you to decide.'

'I'll have a look round,' she said. 'I gave a lift to the neighbour, by the way. Just down from the village, I mean.'

'The sinister Dennis?' I said.

'Not Dennis. This was a woman. Minute white woman with a voice to match.'

'That would be Mrs Wainwright. I've met her once.'

Stella went on walking round the empty rooms. 'I'd like to paint her,' she said. 'No use for a head, I don't think. If she's that colour all over, she'd be wonderful for a nude. The fleshtints would be splendid and she's nicely put together.'

She did not look at me at all. I laughed as best I could. 'I don't know her that well,' I said. 'You'd better ask her yourself. But you'd better have a look at Dennis first. I don't think he'd approve.'

She nodded. 'Only an idea,' she said. 'No hurry. Jake, I can't decide without daylight. I'll doss down where my stuff is for tonight and make up my mind tomorrow.'

'Of course,' I said. 'I'll get your gear out of the car.'

From down in the hall Elizabeth called, 'Stella?'

'Here,' Stella said. 'Coming.' We went downstairs together.

CHAPTER FOUR

Stella chose the second floor and began to spread her things over it in the way she had. She was a great accumulator of minor physical possessions, and established her effective ownership of a place more quickly and thoroughly than anyone I knew. As Elizabeth could not pretend to need any of the second-floor rooms, and had already had a free choice of the first floor, this did not matter. The weather held for a day or two more, and Stella was out on the beach most of the time, trying to capture that vast blue and gold emptiness in very thin paint and cursing steadily under her breath at what she considered her failure to do so. Elizabeth lay in her hide and waited for the exotic visitors she constantly hoped for, and I spent a lot of time in the wood, deciding what should be kept and what got rid of if ever I got my hands on it, and wondering when and where I might come up with Carol Wainwright. We were all, I suppose, happy in a rather restless, half-baked sort of way. Those were the last days of even comparative peace. The weather hung in the balance, waiting for the breakup. So in fact did a great deal else, but we could not know this.

I went into the wood early on the afternoon of the second day after Stella's arrival. With all the landscape bleaching steadily round it, the heavy perennial green of the oak leaves seemed darker than ever, and nothing stirred under them. I went to my hide, but saw nothing. The door of the red-brick house stood open, but there was no sign of life anywhere. I sat down, rather uncomfortably, on a dead branch that was not wide enough for the job and put my head on my arms. I wondered whether I could not break away and achieve some reasonable peace of mind again, but I was already to a frightening extent trapped. Stella had been right about the place, but Stella did not know the half of it. Left to itself, it was a place I could have surrendered to peaceably and let myself in due course be absorbed by. As it was, the whole place was permeated for me by the nagging image of Mrs Wainwright, so that I could neither be at peace there while she was at the other end of the wood, nor break away from it with my luck still untried and the mystery of her still unexplored. The only thing to do, as far as I could see, was to push things, so far as she was concerned, to a point where they fell decisively one way or another. Even if, as the most inglorious result, I simply outgrew my illusions, my life here might become manageable again, whatever it had been in the meantime. The only difficulty was that I found it very hard, at the moment, to push things forward at all. The first meeting, to be of any use, had to be a chance one, even if the chance was to some extent contrived: and at present the chance was not occurring, and I did not know how to engineer one.

I noticed now that the leaves had started to rustle over me. The calm had cracked. The air was beginning to move. I still did not lift my head, but listened, with my head on my arms, to the stir and whisper of the wood all round me. When at last I said, 'Hell,' and looked up, Mrs Wainwright was standing in the path I had made not a couple of yards from me. We looked at each other fixedly for what seemed a very long time. Neither of us smiled at all. There was from the start an almost deliberate rejection of social pretences on either side.

She said, 'You're not a very sensible person, are you? This isn't a very sensible thing to do. Are you very unhappy?' Her voice was just on the edge of kindness, so that I felt neither so completely silly as I ought to have felt nor encouraged to put myself irremediably on her sympathy. I remembered Stella's saying she had a voice to match. It worried me because it accorded with my own observation, and for some reason I shrank from taking over, in Mrs Wainwright's case, the impressions of Stella's accurate, dispassionate mind.

I said, 'Not unhappy. Confused, I admit. Confused as hell. Did you know I was here?' I heaved myself up off my uncomfortable perch, and found that one leg had gone fairly completely to sleep. I staggered, clutched a tree-trunk for support, and stood there, leaning over and rubbing the back of my thigh. We were still looking at each other. It was almost unbelievably unromantic.

'Yes, of course,' she said. 'I've seen you here before. And I've been here when you weren't here. I thought I'd come out and tell you. I didn't think it would be a good idea if Dennis saw you.'

I put the last bit away for further examination later. It gave me a glimmer of warmth, but I did not want to make too much of it. I said, 'Do you come into the wood much, then? I've never seen you.'

She nodded. 'I have at times, yes. I think if we're going to talk I'd rather we went back along the path a bit. Do you mind?' She turned and went off along my twisting track. I said, 'Of course,' and followed her. The circulation had come back into my leg, and I could walk without actually cannoning into things. She went between the crowding hazards like an animal, threading them in her stride without hesitation or apparent contrivance. She was a great deal smaller than I was, but she was still a beautiful mover. After a bit she stopped by one of the trees I knew and turned to face me. Like most of the trees in the wood, it grew slightly off the vertical. She leant back against the slightly leaning stem, feet together, arms crossed in front of her, and looked up at me. I had a moment of something very like panic. I was over the brink now and falling irretrievably. I did not know for certain whether I had ever been in love before, but now at least I was completely at Carol Wainwright's mercy, and did not think I should ever be anything else.

I said, 'Why did your husband buy this wood, do you know? Does he like trees? He doesn't seem to have done much to it so far.'

'I don't know. Do you know why your uncle sold it to him?'

'I don't even know why he left me the house. I had never had anything much to do with him. I don't think I ever set eyes on him after I was at school. He was rather the black sheep of the family, I think. But I never heard what there was against him.'

'He was quite a friend of Dennis's. At least, Dennis used to be round at the Holt House quite a lot. I don't know what they had in common.'

'Straight misanthropy, perhaps.'

'Not exactly. I don't think Dennis is against people. He just doesn't want any more to do with them than he can possibly help. I got the idea your uncle was the same. I thought perhaps they had both been so successful in shutting everyone else out that there were more or less only the two of them left. Do you see what I mean? I don't think Dennis bought the wood because he likes trees. He doesn't particularly. I don't know of anything he does like particularly. But it bulks very large in our landscape. We didn't call the house Holm Oaks, but we haven't called it anything else. I rather imagine that Dennis didn't like the idea of anyone else owning it once your uncle was dead. But what he'll do with it now he's got it I haven't any idea.'

'There's a lot needs doing to it that could still be done. Is he likely to do anything, do you think?'

'Not if it costs money.'

'He wouldn't cut it down?'

'I've told you – I don't know what he'd do. I never have known. About that or anything else.'

'And in the meantime you walk here on occasion?'

'On occasion, yes.'

'Do you mind if I do, too?'

'I don't mind what you do so long as you stop lurking in the trees and gazing at the front of our house.' She spoke, still perfectly seriously, but there was the faintest suggestion of a smile at the corners of her eyes. I said, 'You know—' and then stopped helplessly.

'I don't know anything,' she said. 'But I'll come into the wood at this time tomorrow and walk straight along the centre path. I might meet you, perhaps. But I can't if you're back there by the road, sitting on a fallen branch with your head between your knees, getting pins and needles.'

'I shan't be. I shall be walking along the centre path in the opposite direction to you. We might, as you say, meet. In fact, I don't really see how we can do anything else.'

She left her tree and came over to me and put a hand on my sleeve. She said, 'Don't be unhappy, Mr Haddon. You're no use to anybody if you're unhappy.'

I said, 'Could I be of use to you, for instance, if I'm not?'

She considered this, carefully, for what seemed a very long time. All the time her hand was on my sleeve, and I was looking at the hand, not her face, which was turned down and away from me. The hand was miniature, like the rest of her, and very white, but of no particular delicacy. Subject to its natural limitations of size and strength, it looked very capable. The leaves kept up their stealthy rustle over our heads.

Finally she said, 'I don't know. You might be. I don't really know whether anyone could be. But not if you're going to be unhappy.'

'I shouldn't be then,' I said. 'It goes round in a circle, rather.'

She took her hand off my sleeve and gave me a quick upwards smile. It was the first time she had really smiled at me, leaving aside her proper politeness when we were introduced. It made her look suddenly and disastrously young. She said, 'We'll see, anyhow.' We picked our way back to the main path, nodded gravely to each other, and went our opposite ways. When I came out of the wood, the breeze was blowing steadily from the south-west, and the voice of the sea on the beach had changed already. The sky was still clear overhead, but the horizon, which had been clear for nearly a week, was covered by a climbing grey haze.

The path from the gate to the front door was flagged and the door was open. I was wearing rubber-soled shoes, but had no intention of creeping up on anybody. In point of fact I assumed that Elizabeth and Stella were both out, as they had been when I left. I heard the voices only as I put my foot into the hall. I was going to speak, hesitated at the first words I heard, and stopped dead.

Elizabeth said, 'If it's Jake you're worrying about, you can stop worrying. Jake is quite capable of looking after himself, and always has been.' They were in the sitting-room on the right of the hall.

Stella said, 'It isn't only Jake, Liz. It's both of you. I think you're making a mistake.'

'But I love it here. And if Jake doesn't want to stay, he can sell at any time. You heard him say so.'

'Of course he said so. That doesn't mean he's capable of doing it. Not if he knows you're set on staying. The only thing that will get you out of here is a lead from you now. In six months' time it will be too late.'

'But why? And why should I give him a lead if I don't want to go? What have you got against the place?'

There was silence for several seconds. I stepped back gingerly until I was just outside the door. I could see, as clearly as if I was in the room, Stella staring at her sister with that fixed, direct, rather lowering look of hers. When she spoke, I could still hear her perfectly clearly from where I was. She said, 'I don't think it will do you any good. It's too – too concentrated.'

'I don't know what the hell you're talking about.' Elizabeth's voice was edgy. She could never stand up to Stella's persistence without losing her temper, and Stella got quieter as she got shriller. 'Do you mean we're going to be too much thrown together and get on each other's nerves? Is that what you mean? And what business is it of yours, anyway? There's no need for you to stay here if you don't want to.'

'I know that.' Stella's voice was so low now that I could hardly hear her. 'But Jake can't get away, can he? Not once you're dug in here.'

I went back down the path, as far as I dared without being seen from the window. Then I turned and walked up to the door. If it had been in the least in character, I should have whistled cheerfully, but it would not have been, and I could not think of anything suitable to whistle. Instead I slapped my feet rather noisily on the steps and walked across the hall and straight into the sitting-room.

I thought Elizabeth had been walking down the length of the room away from the door. As I came in, she was standing stock still, her body facing at least three parts away from me, and her head turned to look at me over her shoulder. Her eyebrows were up almost into her hair and her mouth drawn down petulantly at the corners. To anyone who knew her, she was clearly near boiling-point. It always spoilt her looks, but she never learnt. Stella was sitting sideways on the arm of a sofa just inside the door. Her legs were gathered comfortably under her and one hand rested on the back of the sofa. The other hand, her right, hung down where only I could see it. The fingers, slightly paint-stained, were rigid, and the thumb widely separated. Her eyes flicked sideways to me and back again to Elizabeth.

Reluctantly – they were neither of them anxious to surrender the tension they had been so laboriously building up – Stella said, 'Hullo, Jake.'

I did not look at either of them longer or more directly than I could help. I said, 'The weather's on the turn. We've had our St Luke's summer. It will be blowing before morning, I think. Any tea yet?'

Elizabeth revolved slowly till she faced the door, still holding herself very straight. 'I'll get some,' she said. She walked past me and out of the door, and went off along the hall towards the kitchen. I looked at Stella. She shook her head. 'Bad timing,' she said. 'You should have come in five minutes later. Or sooner. But not just then.'

'Oh?' I said. 'Sorry. Would you like me to go out again and let you fight to a finish?'

She shook her head again. 'It's no good,' she said. 'It's never any good. I don't know why I bother to fight at all.' The competence and independence were suddenly and rather shockingly missing, and she looked utterly desolate. Then she got up and put her shoulders back. 'Is it really blowing up?'

she said. 'I'd better go and collect the rest of my gear. I didn't pack up properly.' She hurried out, pulled, as always, by the invisible forces that dragged her after them. I sat down, folded *The Times* to bring the crossword uppermost and began to think about Carol Wainwright.

When Elizabeth brought in the tray she said, 'Where's Stella?'

'I don't know,' I said. 'I think she went to get her stuff in off the beach.'

She nodded, poured out two cups of tea and handed me one. Then she sat down opposite me, looking at me speculatively over the top of her cup.

Twice, to my certain knowledge, she got herself lined up to speak but thought better of it. Then she said, 'Is it really blowing up?' She said it so exactly as Stella had said it that I almost jumped. It was easy, as a rule, to forget how alike their voices were, because they said such different things. It was only when they meant nothing that the likeness came out, and Stella at least very seldom did.

'I think so,' I said. 'The house-warming's over. Now we're going to see what this place can really do.'

I went out after tea and walked in the last of the daylight, not into the wood, which had for the time being lost its mystery, but westwards along the edge of the rising tide. The seas were coming in steadily now in endless lines. They hit the beach a little obliquely, so that the broken water swirled sideways across the grating pebbles before it was sucked back under the feet of the next breaker. It was a mean-looking sea, even with its malice hardly extended.

It was nearly dark before I came back, with the wind half under my tail, to the lights of the house above the beach and the long shadow of the oak-wood stretching away in front. Twice, as I turned to go up what was left of the beach, I thought I heard a shot from further east, but the wind was against it, and I could not be certain.

CHAPTER FIVE

Where I slept, on the east side of the house, you heard the sea, in these conditions, almost more than the wind. There is a lot of comfort in letting a house take the weather round you at night, provided, of course, you do not have to worry about the house. I did not worry about the Holt House at all. For one thing I had already seen too much of it to suspect any weaknesses. For another there was its history and position. It had stood where it was above the beach, turning a stiff back to the prevailing wind, for what looked like two hundred years at least, and it was not going to let the first freshening of autumn wind upset it. I did not sleep much, for other reasons, but I lay snugly enough during the early part of the night and let the wind spend itself on quite unmoving masonry. It was only later that the noise of the sea began to obtrude itself into my consciousness, and once it was in, it was very difficult to get it out. It was quite impossible to shut out physically. It was a steady pulsation that permeated everything. To pull the bedding round my ears brought it home to me more solidly. The only hope was to shut it out of my mind, or at least to let my mind absorb it without comment; and this I found I could not do.

I lay for a very long time, consciously listening to it and, after a bit, consciously wishing it would stop. In the end, of course, I went to sleep, but I woke, tired out and early, to a grey light very different from the daffodil-yellow we had woken to for the past week. It was still too early for Elizabeth. Stella, as in other matters, had no very fixed rules, but I never saw her in the early mornings. I got up, dressed warm and went out on to the beach. It was not, in fact, much before eight, but it felt earlier. It was not blowing hard, not by the standards we learnt to use later, but the whole world was changed and very comfortless. The sea was grey, not yet flecked at all with white, but ridged endlessly with slate-grey advancing crests. They came in on the slant, kicked up over the fierce undertow that came back off the beach, and burst in a smother of white foam and flung pebbles, which sluiced off sideways to undercut the next advancing hummock of grey water. I turned my back to the wind and walked eastwards through the incessant, repetitive tumult that had kept me awake during the night. When I came to the end of the wood, I moved up closer to the edge of the trees. They were still full of darkness, but I found their stability comforting. I walked almost the whole length of the wood, farther, certainly, than I had ever walked along the beach before. The trees blocked all the landward view. Every fifty yards of beach was exactly like the one next to it.

On the beach itself nothing moved at all. Anything the wind could move it had moved during the night, and it blew steadily, without gusts. I was nearly at the far end of the wood when I saw something flopping and lolloping over the pebbles ahead of me. It was coloured like them, grey with black and white touches, and was almost invisible except when it moved. It kept its distance ahead of me. At times I nearly caught up with it, then it would be off again, slithering irregularly over the rounded stones. When I saw, as I came fairly close to it, a momentary flap of wing, I realised it was a dead bird, and ran to catch up with it. When I caught up with it, I realised it was not dead.

It was a tern of sorts, grey with a black cap that had been shot and left. One long swallow-wing was intact and one red leg. The other wing was a crumpled mess. I could not see the other leg at all. The eye was bright, watching me as I came up to where it lay in a tumbled heap on the stones. Then it got under way again with its two sound limbs, doing its best, now it was too late, to keep its distance from man on the beach.

I stopped and tried to think sensibly, but even commonsense told me there was no help for it, and my instinct clamoured to catch it and kill it quick. I had nothing to kill it with but my hands, and perhaps a larger than average pebble. I ran at it, stumbling over the stones in my desperation, but it flapped away under my grabbing hand, and I came down on my knees with the bird still making its systematic, demented way in front of me.

I said, 'Oh God,' and got to my feet again. I think I was almost sobbing. 'Come *here*, sweetie,' I said, 'come *here*,' calling desperately to it to come and be killed for its own comfort and mine. It could not keep away from me for long, and the next time I made sure of it. It was nothing in my hands at all, but the round dark eye still looked sideways at me out of the grey cheek-feathers, and the heart ticked furiously under one of my fingers. I looked up and down the beach, but there was nothing anywhere but a wilderness of grey pebbles between the dark stooping trees and the white breaking edge of the sea.

I said, 'I'm sorry, sweetie,' apologising comprehensively for my race and for what I had to do. Then my fingers closed on its neck, and I shut my eyes and got it over with a convulsive jerk of the wrist. It flapped once as I let it fall, and then lay still. I had to make sure it was dead, but did not want to touch it again for fear it was not. I picked up the largest stone I could find and, standing over the bird, threw it down with all my force at the tucked-in head. The stone missed the head and came down on the spread wing. The whole grey body leapt with the shock and collapsed again. I grabbed at the stone and smashed it savagely down, fairly, this time, on the neat black-capped head. Nothing moved at all. The bird had been dead all along, and now the skull was beaten to a pulp. I piled pebbles over it until nothing showed. Then I turned and went back along the beach, walking into the wind.

I wondered what could be done about people who shot down small sea-birds in the dusk and left them to flap about on the beach all night. My thinking was almost wholly fantastic and not really very creditable. I did not intend to tell Elizabeth and Stella about the bird. It could do no good, and it would hurt them both considerably in different ways. But mainly it was because it was my secret. I assumed, until the contrary was proved, that it was Mr Wainwright who had shot the bird, and my war with him was a private one and fought mainly for reasons Elizabeth could not be expected to approve of. If she came in on my side, the thing would get too mixed altogether. I guarded my hatred of Mr Wainwright from her as jealously as I guarded my love for his wife.

I found breakfast in progress and Stella packed up to go. For the first time, almost, that I could remember, I was glad she was going. In some way I did not examine very closely, she would be more of a difficulty than Elizabeth in the way of whatever developed between Carol Wainwright and myself. I assumed her emotional detachment, but knew that my mind was much more vulnerable to hers. My whole thinking was already dominated by my feelings for Carol Wainwright and, even with next to no evidence to go on, the incident of the bird coloured, and was coloured by, these feelings. It was, substantially, a different woman I went to the wood to meet because of the dead bird under its cairn of grey pebbles on the beach below.

Now that I came to think of it, our appointment was a very vague one. The time for organised assignations and accurate timing had not yet come. Stella went off after breakfast, and I spent the morning alone in a fever of anticipated difficulties and imaginary conversations. Elizabeth and I had lunch in a mood of carefully sustained cheerfulness, and after lunch I went into the wood and walked slowly along the central pathway. I was, in fact, almost exactly half-way along it when I met Carol Wainwright walking slowly in the opposite direction. We neither of us said anything at first. We stopped and stood looking at each other, there in the dark pathway. The trees, so far as we could see them from below, did not move at all, but the invisible tops kept up a steady background of noise. I could not hear the sea. She was muffled from the ears to the calves in a dark red coat that made her look smaller than ever.

I said, 'What was it you asked your husband about, and he said he couldn't find?' I do not know what, after all my considered openings, put this in my head. I suppose it had been worrying me ever since that first evening and of course the worry had grown on me.

She put her hands in the pockets of her coat and stood with her feet a little apart, looking up at me. 'When was this?' she said.

'About three weeks ago, I suppose. At the end of September. In the evening. There was a man singing *Nessun dorma*, and in the middle you called out to your husband and asked him if he had found something. He was outside the door. He said he didn't know where it was.'

'And where were you? Hiding in the wood?' She had coloured very slightly, but her voice was elaborately detached. I shook my head. 'Standing in the road, with my wife. But it was almost dark. It was the first time we came down. I didn't see you, or only for a moment through the window.'

She nodded. 'It was a gramophone record,' she said.

'Yours?'

'Yes. More opera, I'm afraid. Does that shock you?'

'Did you ever find it?'

'No.'

'Why should it shock me?'

She shrugged. 'It does some people. It would have me, once, I think. Only down here—'

'I know,' I said. 'I think I really do know. I was pretty startled by *Nessun* myself.' I had a very clear picture of this small white woman in a grey world, playing Italian opera to herself to keep herself warm. I think if she had not had her hands in her pockets, I should have gone straight to her and taken hold of her.

She smiled suddenly. 'You should have heard *Una furtiva lagrima*,' she said. 'Only that was the one I lost.'

I said, 'You didn't play *Nessun* for very long.'

'Didn't I? Oh no, I remember.' She coloured again. 'Would you like me to show you the wood? I expect you think you know it, but there's more to it than you'd think. There's another main ride, parallel with this one, between this and the beach, and a whole system of cross-rides. It's all overgrown, of course, but it was a careful piece of planting, and the original trees are very complete. It's only the undergrowth and the new stuff that clutter it up.' She turned, still with her hands in her pockets, and went off between the trees southwards towards the beach. She wore quite elegant stockings and what in another woman I should have thought of as sensible shoes. She seemed able to go through the tangle with that even padding walk of hers without collecting snags at every other step. She was not at all the kind of woman one generally describes as feline. She had a lot of cat-like qualities, but they were not the qualities which man for some reason picks on as most characteristically cat-like. She was above all very neat and profoundly economical in all her movements. 'There,' she said, 'do you see?'

There was in fact a gap in the big trees on both sides of us. Now that I came to consider it apart from the intrusive tangle, I could see that there had, as she said, been a ride here, running the length of the wood parallel with the central path. It was filled from side to side with saplings and undergrowth, but the old trees walled it with uncompromising lines and nearly met overhead. Down the middle of what had been the ride, not straight, but picking its way zig-zag through the tangle, there was a well-marked path, very narrow, but beaten firm underfoot and clear above, though hardly to my height. Allowing for the difference in height, it was like the path a wood-animal makes, but I did not think there could be badgers here. I knew who had made it, in fact. Carol Wainwright turned left and went off along it, heading for her end of the wood. I followed as best I could, ducking under the branches that cleared her head and working my way rather noisily through the passage she negotiated with hardly a whisper. If it had not been for the wind in the tops of the trees, you could have heard me moving from fifty yards off. You could not have heard her in a flat calm. She never took her hands out of her pockets. She might have been walking along a rather crowded pavement.

Then the path jinked sideways suddenly, and there was a circular clearing, hardly more than six feet across. One of the original oaks had fallen here and left two logs, just big enough to sit on in comfort, and a couple of feet apart. She waved me to one of them. 'Sit down,' she said. She herself sat on the other. We were not quite facing each other, but near enough.

She sat there with her hands thrust into her pockets, her head sunk into her upturned collar and her sensible shoes neatly disposed side by side. It was cold in the wood when you stopped walking. She smiled at me suddenly out of her coat-collar. It was like a child who on an impulse has let you bodily into one of its chosen secrets. She said, 'We shan't be disturbed here, I think. Now tell me why you have been watching the house.'

I sat there with my legs stuck straight out in front of me. I was too long to sit on my log with her compact tidiness, and I did not want to crouch. I stared between my slightly muddy shoes and saw no means of prevaricating and no reason for prevarication. 'To see you,' I said.

'But why like that?'

'I don't know anything about you, you see. And I was in love with you. I have been in love with you since you came into the room and your husband introduced us. I'm sorry if it seems unreasonable.'

'Don't apologise. I think I like your being in love with me. Only I don't know what I'm supposed to do about it.'

'There's nothing you can do about it. But please let me go on seeing you.'

She said, 'Mr Haddon—'

'Don't you think, as I'm in love with you, you might call me Jake?'

'All right, Jake, then. Do you do this often? I mean meeting strange women in the woods and telling them you are in love with them.'

'I don't do it at all. I haven't been in love with anyone for years now. Let alone told them so.'

She thought about this, looking at me all the time with the slightest smile half hidden in her coat-collar. Then she said, 'Have you really thought what you're doing? Suppose I decide to fall in love with you?'

'I want you to, of course. I want it more than I can remember wanting anything.'

'But you don't know—' She thought again, frowning now and groping for words. 'You don't know anything about me, do you? You've just said so. You don't know what it would mean if I did.'

'I do,' I said. 'I know that much already. It would be all or nothing. But the whole place is all or nothing, and here I am.'

'You know that, do you? That's something, anyhow.' She thought again. 'I'm a worse case than you. I've never loved anybody, not since I was a child.'

'Don't you think it's time you did?'

'It's time, all right, high time. Too high for comfort. That's what you've got to think about.'

'I have thought. I was thinking yesterday when you walked in on me. Or trying to think. I wasn't being very successful. I'm past thinking about it, Carol. The only question for me is whether I hadn't better go now.'

'You mean away from here altogether?'

'Yes. Sell the house at once. Cut my losses, I suppose. I can't go on as I am.'

She got up suddenly, throwing the collar back clear of her face and looking down at me with immense seriousness. The illusion of childishness had gone completely. She did not even, seen like this, look a particularly young woman. The skin was flawed round the eyes and under the throat. I sat still on my log with my legs thrust out in front of me, but if I had been prostrate on my face, I could not have been more completely at her mercy.

She shook her head, very slowly, without taking her eyes off my face. I did not know whether she was shaking it at me or at herself.

'Don't do that,' she said. 'Not yet, anyhow. I must think. Let me go now.'

I got up and we walked back to the central path without another word said. There she touched my arm once and left me. I hardly remember leaving the wood, but I remember how the noise of the sea burst on me quite suddenly as I came out of it. I know I did not go into the house at all, but walked along the beach westward into the still freshening wind.

CHAPTER SIX

The cheerfulness of lunch continued over tea, and needed less maintaining. I was myself in a curiously light-headed mood. Tremendous waves of exultation went through me like electric charges, so that I wanted to snap my fingers and wave my arms in time to unheard melodies even when I was holding a teacup or cutting myself a slice of cake. Underlying these, and emerging when they faded temporarily, was a desperate impatience bordering on despair. I was aware, all the time, of appalling and inevitable decisions that stood between me and the consummation of a suddenly apprehended and almost unbelievable happiness. My mind was totally unconditioned to emotions of this intensity, and behaved with the bewildering unreliability of a sedentary body suddenly involved in long forgotten exercise. I noticed, but did not mind, an inconsequentiality in what I said that must have bordered on incoherence.

Elizabeth was still in the state of barely suppressed exhilaration which she always experienced, and was seldom able to disguise, when Stella had left us, and found in my mood an answer to her own that did not require further explanation. I doubt if two people so completely at cross purposes ever got on so well. There was a monstrous instability in the whole relation that avoided collapse by its own inherent momentum. She was full of plans to get the distressing, but certainly unmistakable, exclamation of *nycticorax* on to the tape as incontrovertible proof of his presence with us.

'The wood is the place,' she said. 'That's his fixed spot, and he's away from it all night, I imagine. If only I can find where he lies up, I can get the recorder rigged up when he's out shopping and then, with any luck, switch on early next evening without disturbing him. Then if he gives tongue when he's getting up, as he seems to do, I've got him.'

I saw no reason, now, to head her off our end of the wood at that hour of the evening. 'We'll have to picket the wood at dusk,' I said. 'If we take up positions just inside the trees and fairly well spaced out, we might both hear him. Then if we each move towards where the sound seems to come from until we meet, we oughtn't to be far off the spot. Then the next night we can close in on him a bit. It may take a night or two, but sooner or later one of us is bound to be almost up to him when he performs. Or near enough, anyhow, to get a recording the next evening if we plant the recorder wherever we are. It can't be far off the central path, because I was coming along it when he flew right over me. You still haven't heard him out on the mere?'

'Not yet, no. He may not actually feed there. Or perhaps he doesn't talk when he's feeding. No, the wood's the place. Do you mind if we have a go this evening? I don't think time is on our side, and I couldn't bear to let him get away from me.'

'All right. It's not going to be so easy with this wind. It was dead quiet when we heard him the first time. But then we were out on the beach. It's much quieter in the wood, even with the wind, and I should think he makes quite a noise when you get up to him.'

We put the tea things away, muffled ourselves in heavy coats and set out on our hunt. When we came to the end of the path, we separated and disposed ourselves about twenty yards on each side of it and just inside the trees. The light was going fast. There should not be too long to wait. If we had not heard *nycticorax* by the time it was fully dark, we were not going to hear him at all. I settled myself as dry and comfortable as possible and tried to think coherently.

I thought entirely about Elizabeth. I could no longer think about Carol Wainwright at all. She was part of my thinking mind and would not be considered objectively. I did not know what I could do about Elizabeth. I knew what I wanted to do, or rather what I had to do. I did not know whether I was capable of doing it. The main trouble was that I did not know, if I did what I had to do, what it would mean to her. Being married to anyone for any considerable time is an almost fatal bar to understanding them. What you know is a relationship, and it is next to impossible to see behind it to the person who would be there if the relationship did not exist. To see ourselves as others see us, whether or not it would ever make a particularly acceptable gift, is, I suspect, child's play compared with seeing one's wife as others see her. The only thing I had against Elizabeth was that she got in my hair and, now that I was no longer fond of her, got in my way. I did not wish her any harm, and I shrank abjectly from the idea of inflicting serious pain on her. But I genuinely did not know how serious the pain would be.

The wind died momentarily out of the leaves, and somewhere in the wood, rather over to my left, something woke up and made a noise like a man being sick. It was not very loud or very near. I doubt whether, but for the lull in the wind, I should have heard it at all. But there was no mistaking it. The excitement of the hunt gripped me suddenly. I got up, straightened myself cautiously, took my torch out of my pocket and set off in the direction of the sound.

It was nearly dark now. I moved laboriously on as straight a bearing as I could. I wondered whether Elizabeth had heard him and was on the move too. As far as I could, I kept an eye upwards, but it was not *nycticorax* himself I was looking for. I was really looking for Elizabeth, coming in on her cross-bearing, and I was undecided how far I ought to go if I did not meet her. It was, as I had told her it would be, much quieter in the wood than it was outside, and uninhibited movement – we had no particular reason to be quiet – ought to be audible at a little distance. Also, I expected her to be using her torch, as I was myself, and it should be possible to see a moving light, even if only at intervals, some time before our courses converged. I plunged on through the thicket, still hoping to meet her coming in on my left, but of necessity chiefly concerned to hold a reasonably direct course towards where, a minute ago, I thought *nycticorax* had been. I had an uncomfortable feeling that our stratagem, which had seemed so simple and water-tight over tea, was not going to stand up to practice in a now nearly pitch-dark wood.

I saw the light first to my left, which I had expected, but some way ahead of me, which I had not. It was only a flicker, but there was no doubt about it. I stopped and thought. If Elizabeth was already so far ahead of me, my line might cross hers behind the point she had already reached, and the important thing was to stop her. 'Elizabeth!' I shouted. 'Elizabeth! Stay where you are. I'm coming.'

I was startled by the noise I made. If *nycticorax* had not already gone, he would be off now as fast as his rather laborious flight could carry him. The silence closed in threateningly and completely. Nothing replied. I was in two minds whether to hold on my previous course or to make for where I had seen the light. 'Elizabeth!' I shouted again. 'Don't go any further. Wait where you are.' I broke into a blundering run, stumbled over a branch, recovered myself, and came out almost at once into what could only be the central path. There was no sign of Elizabeth anywhere. I stood still and listened. The wind swished continuously in the tops of the trees, and I myself breathed rather more noisily than my short burst of energy seemed to justify. I could not, against this background, hear any movement anywhere.

I began to follow the path eastwards, and was aware, almost at once, that someone was moving along it ahead of me. They were some way ahead, and moving faster than I was, at what sounded like a rather hurried walk. I gathered myself to shout again, but at once thought better of it. Whoever was on the path ahead, it could not surely be Elizabeth. Unless the excitement of the chase had tipped her right off balance, there was no conceivable reason why she should either make off along the path like that or fail to reply to my shouts. And whoever it was on the path must have heard me.

I did not like it. It was not, whatever I felt about it, my wood, and I had in fact no right to be anywhere in it, at night or at any other time, except where I now was, following my right-of-way along the central path. Something of the poacher's guilt affected me, and I badly wanted to get back over the line into my own ground. At the same time, I resented what seemed to be a surreptitious intrusion on my privacy. I did not like plunging about a dark wood at night, calling loudly to my wife, in the presence of an unknown observer. But basically I think I was afraid. Not logically, because a person who seems determined to keep his distance cannot on the face of it be very dangerous. But underlying my indignation was a purely primitive horror of the night walker, *noctu perambulans*, the thing that lurks in the trees and does not come out when you call to it. And I still did not know where Elizabeth was.

I had already switched off my torch. Now I stood still again and listened. I thought I heard the movements again ahead of me, but I could not be certain. If they were there, they were fainter. Whoever it was was probably moving out of earshot. I turned and went straight back along the path, refusing to switch my torch on again, and trying not to run. I think if *nycticorax* had chosen that moment to cough up immediately overhead, I should hardly have checked my stride for him. The pleasurable excitement had gone out of the night's work, and all I wanted was to get home to a lit room and a drink.

The sound of the sea hit me, as it always did, as I came to the end of the path. The thing I most remember now about all that time, but did not consciously notice then, is the way the sound of the sea on the beach, which never left us, built up steadily, until it came to form a continuous background to everything any of us did or said. Only in the middle of the wood, throughout all the time, was it ever properly quiet; and the middle of the wood is not the place I choose to remember.

I turned to the right along the edge of the wood, opened my mouth to shout and was picked out immediately in the steady glare of a torch.

'Jake? Did you hear anything?'

'Yes. Didn't you? Very faint, but fairly definite. I followed the line as far as the path. Then I realised you hadn't come, so I came back.'

'Damn. Oh damn.' She sounded dreadfully disappointed.

'Have you got anything to go on, do you think?'

'Not much. I should say about fifty yards along the path and then a bit off to the right. Let's get in, shall we? I need a drink.'

'All right. I tell you what. Tomorrow evening I'm going to put the recorder where you say and lie up near it myself. If we're near enough, I may get him first time. If he speaks up within earshot, but too far for a recording, I'll shift the recorder nearer. It's the same idea, only short-circuited a bit. We started too far out tonight.'

'We had to start somewhere. And at least we know he's there and have some idea where he is.' I was not thinking about *nycticorax* at all. We walked back side by side, with the wind blowing steadily in our faces and the sea-noises rising and falling round our heads, as far apart mentally as if we lived at opposite ends of the seven-mile beach and had never met. My mind was full, as Elizabeth's was, of what I had met in the wood that evening and what I hoped I should meet there tomorrow. But neither of these was *nycticorax*. She talked incessantly, and with the terrible and instinctive skill of long propinquity I kept up my end of the conversation and thought of what Carol Wainwright would look like, and what she would say, and whether I should ever get over the complete and instantaneous devastation of her sudden upwards smile. The lit hall showed Elizabeth flushed and anxious, and I saw with a faintly regretful but quite resigned detachment that she was still, at times, a beautiful woman. We waved our glasses cheerfully at each other, but I did not know clearly what I was drinking to, and I am certain Elizabeth did not.

I slept even worse than I had the night before, and all night the sea pounded on the beach. It has two rhythms, the incessant, almost momentary beat of the waves and the vastly slower advance and retreat of the tides. Only a long and concentrated session of night-listening established the second in one's consciousness. The beach was a steep one, and the lateral movement of the breaking line was not large. But it was recognisable, and served to intensify the timelessness that is the wicked essence of real insomnia. I did not much care for the look of myself in the morning, and wondered whether Elizabeth would notice anything, but she had slept soundly and woken up full of fresh and beautiful ideas for catching *nycticorax*, and my misery was lost on her. This had irritated me so often in the past that it needed a conscious effort of the will to remind myself that now I did not want her to notice anything, and that her sympathy, even if I had it, would be nothing but an embarrassment. Both being, in our own way, anxious to bundle time away, we agreed to go shopping in the morning, and took the car to Burtonbridge, where the shops were still new enough to be entertaining, and we had yet to find the best places for coffee and butcher's meat. Elizabeth got lost in the ornithological section of the County Library, and was mildly surprised at my feverish impatience to be back at the usual time for lunch.

At lunch she got on to the subject of Stella's painting, which I did not understand very well myself, but certainly understood a lot better than Elizabeth. This was familiar ground for manoeuvre. She had two standard openings: 'I can't think why she doesn't—' and 'It always seems to me that—'. Regardless of what followed, in the first case I could always think of a dozen good reasons why she should not, and in the second whatever always seemed to Elizabeth never seemed to me. Elizabeth knew this perfectly well, and was secure of the best of both worlds. If I could be drawn into explanation or defence, she would have the righteous satisfaction of thinking, even if she did not say, that Stella talked to me more than she did to her (which of course was perfectly true), and that my ability to explain or wish to defend was in some obscure way an affront to her. If I refused to be drawn, she was left to air her opinions, knowing that they irritated me as much as they would have irritated Stella, but that I was less technically equipped to rebut them and in any case strategically inhibited from doing so. She never, in fact, or only in extreme cases, complained of anything Stella did to Stella herself. She complained to me, not because she expected me to do anything about it, but because her indignation when I did not somehow compensated her for the wrong she thought she had suffered at Stella's hands.

The one thing Elizabeth never suspected was that on this occasion my refusal to be drawn was, virtually for the first time, based on genuine indifference. I was in a fever to be off to the wood, and could not be bothered with either my wife or my sister-in-law. When I eventually got away, I was twenty minutes later than I had been on the last two afternoons. The fact that I had no understanding with Carol Wainwright to meet her at any particular time, or indeed to meet her at all, meant next to nothing to me. I had to be there in case.

I walked the whole length of the central path in growing distress and did not meet her. When I came to the far end, I looked cautiously from the shelter of the trees at the blank face of the red brick house, but could see nothing and nobody. I walked all the way back and then, not knowing what else I could do, turned to walk eastwards again. I was half-way back when a hope born of desperation turned me southward towards the overgrown ride and the small twisting run that zig-zagged along its centre. I went regardless now, blundering through the obstacles in my almost intolerable anxiety, until the track jinked suddenly and I was in the circular clearing. Carol Wainwright sat with her back to me on one of the fallen logs. She must have heard me coming from some way back, but for a long second she still sat there and I stood silent watching her back. Then she seemed to take a breath and, getting up, almost ran to me, holding out both her hands.

CHAPTER SEVEN

I have no intention of recording in detail the progress of my affair with Carol Wainwright. When she had talked about deciding to fall in love with me, she had meant exactly what she said. She always knew what was happening to her better than anyone I have ever known. She was ready, even over-ready, to fall in love with someone, and she decided to let it be me. If this sounds cold-blooded, I can only say that there was in my experience very little cold blood in her. She stepped deliberately into the current, not knowing, as she had warned me, how fast or how far it would take her. It took her very fast and very far.

I myself at this time lived in a fever of alternating ecstasy and despair which makes it very difficult for me to get, at this distance, a reasonable picture of what it was really like. What I must make clear, partly in my own justification and partly to make sense of what followed, is that there was none of the smug excitement of the bored husband who discovers a complaisant young farmer's wife in the next village, and wonders how far he can run things without upsetting the applecart. On the contrary, I had found, beyond all expectation, the only woman I could bear to spend the rest of my life with; and I was appalled both at the thought of giving her up and at the thought of what would be involved if I did not. In the meantime, we both accepted that secrecy was essential. So far as the mechanics of the thing went, it might have been the farmer's wife. If the cynic finds cause for amusement in this, let him live through what I lived through and keep smiling.

We met, as we had first met, in the wood, which Carol knew by heart and in detail. 'I've spent half my time here,' she said. 'The garden is Dennis's, and I don't like the beach, except when it's hot and still. There's no peace to be had. But no one ever came into the wood, not in your uncle's time.'

'The first time I saw you, you asked me whether I had come through the wood. I wondered why.'

'I had to know, don't you see? I had to know whether you were the sort of person who would choose to walk through the wood rather than come round by car.'

'And were horrified when I said I had? You didn't look it. You didn't look anything. You just nodded.'

'Not horrified, Jake. If you had been anyone else – but with you it was an additional qualification.'

'Does your husband know what the wood means to you?' I could never bring myself to call him Dennis when I was talking to Carol. With Elizabeth, who at this stage had still not met him, he could be Dennis or our Dennis, but not with Carol. I avoided, as far as I could, mentioning him at all. If I had to, I talked about her husband. It rubbed an extra grain or two of salt in the wound every time I did it, but for some reason it made the thing less like the farmer's wife.

She said, 'I don't know. I hope not.'

'I wondered if that was why he bought it.'

Her head had been against me, but now she twisted away suddenly and looked me in the face. Her eyes were very wide open but the whole face deliberately blank. 'What do you mean?' she said.

'Well, what I said. Nothing complicated. I thought he might have bought it because he knew you liked it. We agreed it was an odd thing for him to do.'

She said, 'I hope to God not.' And that was all I could get out of her.

Presently she pushed me away and said, 'I must go and get tea.' She has quite decisive and matter-of-fact about it. Our time together was demarcated for us by the hours of Dennis Wainwright's meals. Elizabeth was much more interested in *nycticorax*'s movements than in mine, and would not have minded much when I came in during the day, but in fact our life at the Holt House moved in a curious and unconscious harmony with the life they lived at the other end of the wood, and I seldom had a late arrival to explain. The fact that I ate very little apparently went unnoticed. The fact that I slept, or seemed to sleep, hardly at all was, of course, my own affair. In any but the very young it takes an awful lot of sleeplessness to produce any marked physical symptoms.

Carol came and went, not by the main path, but by devious tracks of her own which brought her out at various points near the southeast corner of the wood. I made my way back to the central path. I was always conscious of a sense of relief when I got there, as if to regain my physical right-of-way somehow neutralised what had happened when I left it. I cannot, and never could, find the least glimmer of logic in this, but I know that if Carol had come to meet me in what was my wood, and not her husband's, the atmosphere would have been very different. What his own view on his proprietary rights were I did not, of course, know. I never saw him: and even if I had, he was a man, both on Carol's account of him and to my own observation, who would guard his views on almost any subject as though they were an obscene secret – which on some matters they very likely were. I believed myself that he walked in the wood at night, or at least had done so on one occasion. I did not mention this to Carol, because I knew it would worry her, and because in any case I did not, as I have said, mention her husband to her more than I could possibly help. It was not in fact until I had met her three or four times that I saw him again at all; and that was in the wood; and by daylight.

Carol had taken herself away from me in that curiously abrupt and decisive way she had, that contrasted so oddly with her behaviour when she was with me, and slipped off through the thicket with hardly a rustle, making for the beach and the bottom of the tarmac road. I forced my way up towards the path, moving confusedly through the haze of exultation and loss she generally left me in. As I got nearer the path I made less and less attempt to go quietly. I was in fact talking to myself audibly, though probably hardly above a whisper.

> *'J'aime ta voix, j'aime l'étrange*
> *Grâce de tout ce que tu dis.*
> *Ó ma rebelle, ô mon cher ange,*
> *Mon enfer et mon paradis.'*

One of the many things I still do not know about Dennis Wainwright is whether he understood French – my French, anyhow. He was standing in the path, not five yards from the point where I came out on to it. He had evidently heard me coming, and was standing stock-still, waiting for me, or at any rate waiting to see who it was. He wore, of all things, breeches and gaiters and carried what might not unfairly have been called a cudgel. He was still smiling at his unexplained joke, looking at me under his heavy brows with his head slightly lowered. He would have been a formidable figure in anyone's eyes. To me, at that particular moment and in those particular circumstances, he looked almost unbelievably sinister.

He did not say anything. For my part, my instinct to have as little to do with the man as possible was strengthened by the fact that I could not think of anything suitable to say. But I could not ignore him altogether, and I was in any case un-willing, for reasons I did not examine, to turn my back on him. I therefore turned and walked slowly up the path towards him. By this time I had got my wits back, and I smiled, not, I think, pleasantly but resolutely, into his smile. When we were about a yard apart, the limits of social tolerance snapped and he spoke. He said, 'Good afternoon, Mr Haddon. Have you been exploring my property?'

'Yes,' I said. My smile was now really pleasant. 'Yes, I have. To tell you the truth, I had formed the impression, rightly or wrongly, that you did not take very much interest in it.'

Without raising his head at all, he shook it, very slowly, from side to side. It could pass, I suppose, for a negative head-shake, but the effect was so startlingly animal that I almost expected him to charge at any moment. Instead he moved his hands, stick and all, behind his back and stood there looking down on me. I stopped just in front of him. I remember thinking quite consciously that he could not, at that range, reach me with his stick without moving his feet.

He said, 'Oh yes? Wrongly, I'm afraid. I take a considerable interest in what belongs to me. Of course, you weren't to know that.'

I nodded. 'Quite so,' I said. 'Still, I could not help wondering what made you decide to buy this wood, and whether you have any plans for it.'

'The wood? I have not had the wood very long, you know. I am considering plans for it, certainly.'

I knew it was no good, but I thought even his reaction might make the question worth while. I said, 'You would not consider selling it to me, I suppose? I am very interested in forestry, and should be glad to have the chance of seeing what I could do with it.'

I should, of course, have known better than to expect to get any satisfaction from observing Dennis Wainwright's reaction to this or anything else. There was, visibly, none, except that he reverted to his previous trick of seeming to weigh exhaustively his answer to a question which could obviously have only one. Finally he said, 'Oh no, Mr Haddon. I could not consider that at all.'

'No?' I said. 'Well, I thought it was worth asking you. I shall be interested to see how your plans develop.'

He nodded. I am not sure whether he had ever quite stopped smiling, but now certainly the smile was there. I did not like it any better than I ever had. He said, 'I'm sure you will. In the meantime—' he brought his hands quite suddenly from behind his back. The stick was as big as ever. 'In the meantime, Mr Haddon, I hope we shall manage to respect each other's property.'

I bowed. I was still watching the stick. 'Speaking for myself,' I said, 'you can be sure of it.'

He hesitated. Heaven forbid that I should make any claim to have been left in possession of the field, but he did have his moment of visible uncertainty. Then he bowed, very slightly, in return, and turned and went off towards his end of the wood. I watched him for a moment. He walked quite quickly, but there was a rigidity about the back which I did not think could be quite natural. I tried to remember the footsteps I had heard going off along the path after our first abortive attempt on *nycticorax*, but I could make nothing of the comparison. To watch him longer seemed a concession I was unwilling to make, and I turned to go. I wondered where Carol had got to, and whether she was by now clear of the wood; but there was nothing I could do about it, and I kept on walking.

When I came to the gate I found Carol and Elizabeth walking side-by-side down the path to meet me. I realised afterwards that if Carol had left the wood by the shortest path and walked straight along the top of the beach, there was no difficulty in her reaching the Holt House well before me, especially after my encounter with her husband. But I had got it so much into my head that she had gone back to the red brick house, that the sight of her on our pathway, talking to Elizabeth, nearly stopped my heart. They were talking very pleasantly. As I appeared at the gate, they both flicked their eyes up momentarily, took me in, and then went on with their conversation. There was no change of expression or visible reaction at all. I had seen women do this before and always found it a little unnerving, but to undergo it from my wife and the woman I loved was shattering.

For the second time in almost a matter of minutes I marched steadily up to an unknown quantity, collecting my wits for the social encounter which physical proximity, if nothing else, was bound to bring on. At exactly the same moment Elizabeth said, 'Hullo, Jake,' and Carol gave me her social smile. 'You have met each other, haven't you?' Elizabeth said. 'Mrs Wainwright has looked in to make my acquaintance.'

'I was walking along the beach,' Carol said, 'and it seemed less than civil to go past without turning in. But I must go now. I have my husband's tea to get.' She looked at me, for a moment, between the eyes with the faintest flicker of her real smile.

I thought two could play surprises. 'I've just been talking to your husband,' I said. 'He was in the wood, and we met as I was coming along.' I repented the moment I had said it, because the shot went home much harder than I had ever intended it should. The reaction was always the same. Her eyes flew open and her face froze. All she said was, 'Oh? Then he'll be wanting his tea.'

They walked on down the path, the tall rose-and-gold woman and the small ivory-and-ebony one, and I stood still by the door and let them go. Their voices were utterly different. I have said, I think, that Elizabeth and Stella were totally unlike except for their voices. Here, for all the obvious physical contrast, there was more difference in the voice than in almost anything else. I have made no fist at all of trying to describe Carol's voice, but to me it was the key thing about her. I suppose that was why I had come out of the wood murmuring '*J'aime ta voix*', to the still doubtful edification of Dennis Wainwright. Elizabeth had never learnt to use her voice properly. It shifted too much with the shifting wind of her thought. Stella, as I have said, had the same voice, but used it very differently. Carol's was an altogether different instrument.

When Elizabeth came back from the gate, she looked at me doubtfully. I have no doubt something had got through to her on one of the various levels of extra-sensory perception women go in for, but she was not reading it loud and clear. There was just something that gave her momentary pause. The top layers of her mind had noticed nothing special about Carol. I wondered, almost desperately, what Carol had made of her, because I had no doubt this was of the utmost importance. But it must wait. Elizabeth said, 'I think she's rather nice, don't you? Not very forthcoming, but very pleasant. Much better than one might have expected from the house, anyway.'

'Yes,' I said, 'that was my impression. Not giving much away, but quite friendly disposed. The husband's a different matter.'

'I think I must see this monster. Shall I ask them to dinner?'

I could think, off-hand, of few more appalling prospects than entertaining the Wainwrights to dinner. It was also, I think, true that a good look at Dennis might make Elizabeth think harder about Carol. I said, 'Better have a quick look at him first. Then if you're sure you want to ask them it's up to you. So far as I'm concerned, I'm quite happy to leave then at the far end of the wood, despite the apparent pleasantness of Mrs Wainwright.'

'All right. I'll do a return drop-in on her, and then perhaps I'll see him. It would be nice to have someone we could ask in, don't you think?' She looked at me doubtfully again. Elizabeth's social urges were unpredictable. There were times when she wanted no company but the birds, but other, luckily intermittent, patches when the, I suppose, formal feminine wish to entertain and be entertained reasserted itself. The difficulty, as far as I was concerned, had always been to spot the onset of a social urge and guide it into fairly congenial channels. Otherwise, there was no knowing whom I might find myself suddenly called upon to help entertain.

'Yes,' I said. 'We ought to make the effort to find some company here, I suppose. It's always a slow business in rather remote places like this. But you want to be doubly careful. Once get yourself saddled with the wrong company, and they're on your backs for the rest of time, unless you're prepared to risk bad blood by choking them off. Anyway, have a look at our Dennis and see what you think.'

'I'll do that. Oh, by the way, Stella's coming tomorrow. Did I tell you?'

'Oh? No.' I did not add 'Good.' I did not want Stella back yet, any more than Elizabeth did.

'She hasn't been away long, has she, this time?'

'Doesn't seem so. I suppose it's the best part of a week.'

Elizabeth was looking at me doubtfully again. She said, 'You'll be glad to have her to talk to, anyhow.' Then she went into the house.

CHAPTER EIGHT

Stella got out of the car and said, 'My God, Jake, what have you been doing to yourself? You look as if you hadn't slept for a week.' She shook her hair back into the rampaging wind and stared at me fixedly. Then she jerked her head towards the sea. 'Does it go on like this all the time?' she said.

'Pretty well. But I don't think it keeps one awake. It's just that if one is awake, one notices it.'

'That I can well believe. What does Liz say?'

'About what?'

'About what the place is doing to you. Or hasn't she noticed?'

'I don't think it's really the place. Not entirely, anyway. I don't think, in fact, we've discussed it.'

To say that Stella sniffed is perhaps not quite fair. She lifted her head and took a short, sharp breath, as if to say immediately and violently what she thought; but in fact she said nothing. Instead she grabbed her case out of the car and started in at the gate.

I said, 'Stella,' and she stopped short and turned back to me. I wanted very badly indeed, at that moment, to tell her about Carol Wainwright and the dilemma I was in, but my instinct stopped me. What I actually said was, 'I don't dislike this place, you know. It doesn't make me unhappy being here.'

She put her suitcase down where it was and walked back to me. She put a hand out, thought better of it and stood there facing me with her hands dangling rather helplessly in front of her. I do not think, now I come to consider it, that I ever actually touched Stella, except for the inevitable accidental contact. She said, 'Well, what is making you unhappy? Something is. You've grown a whole fresh set of lines in a week. You've got to get away from here, Jake.'

'Don't you think that's for me to decide?'

'Oh, it's for you to decide all right. But I don't think you'll make the right decision. Not in competition with *nycticorax* and a gaggle of visiting geese.'

'I'm not in competition with *nycti*. I'm rather fond of him, actually. He has his uses, you know.'

'I know that. But are you bound to go through whatever it is you're going through?'

'I'm trying to decide,' I said.

She took her eyes off me and turned back to her suitcase. 'It's no good,' she said. 'It never has been any good.' She picked up her suitcase and went on into the house. I heard her calling 'Liz! Liz!' in the hall and up the stairs, but I knew Elizabeth was out. There was nothing I could do, and I turned and went off towards the wood. I had no reason to think Carol could be there at that time, but at least it would be quiet there, quieter than anywhere else unless you went a mile or so inland.

The noise of the sea died away behind me as I went along the central path, but there was to be no quiet in the wood either. As soon as I got near the far end of the path, I heard men's voices ahead of me. I stopped and listened. I was not sure, but I thought they were coming towards me. I turned aside into the trees and waited for them, but after a bit I decided that they were stationary at or near the far end of the wood. I went back to the path and made my way cautiously along it. I still could not tell who they were or what they were saying. I believe I could pick out Dennis Wainwright's rumble alternating with lighter, local voices, but this may be wisdom after the event. I certainly never heard anything that was said.

You could not see far along the path at any point. It had been straight enough to start with, but it was being grown into from both sides, and the clear line was seldom perfectly straight now for very long. But the main thing was that it undulated. The slope of the land to the shore was seamed with drainage lines and shallow dips, and the path cut straight across them, plunging up and down like a miniature scenic railway. At two of the deeper drainage lines, which were more or less chronically wet, it was carried on low culverts with earthenware pipes under them. At the rest it merely dived into a greener hollow, where the foot hesitated for a moment in softer soil before it climbed again on the harder slope beyond. One way and another, it was seldom possible to see much further than twenty yards ahead. You could go quietly enough, which off the path was very difficult; but once admit the possibility of a menace in the wood, and you went very cautiously from sighting-point to sighting-point. The last sighting-point was daylight on the tarmac. Until that came, the next kink in the path might bring you to anything.

I went very cautiously indeed until I realised that now the voices were going away in front of me. Then I hurried, but by the time I saw daylight they had gone altogether, and a car had started up and moved off up the road. I did not go right to the end. I turned, and had not gone fifty yards back along the path when I heard Carol calling, 'Jake! Jake!' from among the trees on my left. I turned and went straight to her, crashing through the thicket regardless until I had her in my arms.

She said, 'Did you see anybody?'

I shook my head. 'It was your husband, wasn't it? Who was with him?'

'I don't know. There were two of them. They came in a car, and he went straight out to them, and they all went into the wood together. I came in along the beach as soon as I could, but I never got near them. I don't like it, Jake. He's never had anyone in the wood before.'

'Was there nothing to show who they were? Did you see the car?'

'Yes, but nothing special about it. A Ford, I think, with a local number. Not a van or anything. Did you really meet him in the wood yesterday?'

I nodded. 'Just after I left you. He was waiting on the path. Didn't he tell you?'

'No. But that doesn't mean anything. What did he say, Jake?'

'I asked him about the wood. I actually asked him whether he'd sell it to me, but he said he had other plans for it. Then he more or less shook his club at me and told me to keep off his property altogether. I still don't know what that was meant to include. And he didn't mention any of this to you at all?'

'No, but then he wouldn't anyhow. He never tells me anything if he can help it. Jake, I don't think I like your wife much. Do you mind?'

I shook my head and said, 'I should have thought that made things easier all round,' but I knew the tone was wrong, and Carol laughed at me. 'Poor Jake,' she said. 'You have all the proper attitudes, haven't you? I can't help it. And yes, of course it makes things easier. But I don't think she really knows you exist. Or only intermittently, when there are no geese about. I don't know whether it's always been like that.'

'It's difficult to remember. It all seems a very long time ago. But I know I never felt her existence as I feel yours. You're part of the air I breathe here. Or the noise of the sea, or something. You pervade everything.'

She gave me her quick upward smile. 'I wonder how far the pervasiveness extends inland. No, don't bother to protest. You don't know, that's the truth. You haven't tried. But I think that's fair enough for a man. Women don't go for places on the same scale, not generally. To me you're as much part of me as my right hand. If you were cut off, there'd still be a ghost you. It would take me quite a long time to persuade myself it wasn't real.'

'I don't intend to be cut off,' I said.

'I know, I know. But we needn't meet much, socially, need we? I shouldn't like it at all.'

'I don't think so. My wife talked of asking you to dine. I tried to head her off by giving her a horrific account of your husband.'

'Oh for God's sake, no, Jake. Head her off at all costs.'

'Would your husband frighten her off, in fact?'

'I don't know. I've told you – I never know. It would depend, I think.'

'On whether he suspected anything?'

She turned me, suddenly, a blank face. 'He mustn't,' she said. 'No, I mean it would depend on what he felt like. He can be quite charming when he wants to, you know.'

'It must be a pretty sinister charm.'

'Well, your wife might like that.' She smiled up at me again. 'It would make a change,' she said. 'You are not at all sinister, Jake. And why in the world,' she said a moment later, 'a man should mind being told he is not sinister is really beyond the wit of woman to understand. It's not a reflection on your virility, Jake darling. I don't want you to be sinister. I've had all of that I can bear. Can't you see that? I must go. I only came out to see what was going on. Later, perhaps.' She pulled my face down and kissed me. Then she was off. I walked back under the shifting roof of leaves until the noise of the surf came in to meet me along the path. I felt the wind on my face a few seconds before I heard, carried on the wind, the sound of women shouting at each other in voices that were far too much alike.

I was conscious simultaneously of a determination not to get involved and a strong wish to know as far as possible what course the quarrel was taking. I knew that if she suffered defeat, as she usually did, Elizabeth would before long vent her baffled indignation on me, and I needed both the right to claim ignorance of the issues involved and a knowledge of the weaknesses of her position. Otherwise I should have to choose, when the storm broke, between a suspect and probably provoking silence and some sort of a commitment on which I should infallibly, when the occasion next arose, be misrepresented to Stella. My position was an ignoble one but, to me at least, apparently unavoidable. I went to the gate, placed the quarrel in the sitting-room on the right as you went into the front door, and turned behind the skirting wall to that side of the house.

As I came close to the end window I heard Elizabeth say, 'You've no right, don't you see? It's not your business and you've no right to say it.'

'Anybody's got a right to say what's true. Being married to a man doesn't give you the right to burke the truth about him. And you know it's true. You know it as well as I do. Or if you don't, you ought to. It's obvious enough, if you'd give Jake a fraction of the attention you give the geese.'

'And who the hell are you to tell me how much attention to give my husband? Why can't you get a proper husband of your own and turn your attention to him instead of being so solicitous about mine?'

There was a moment's pause and then Stella said very slowly and very clearly, 'You're a vulgar little thing, aren't you, Liz? It's Daddy's side of the family. He didn't do us badly, but he was a vulgar little man, God rest his soul. I suppose that's where you get it from. You've always had it, ever since I can remember. You've only got to let your hair down a bit, and out it pops. I imagine it was rather attractive when you were younger. A touch of vulgarity can be. But it's wearing a bit thin now. Don't you think it's time you stopped reducing everything to the lowest possible level? It doesn't help to settle anything. Let's forget me and my spotted spinsterhood and get back to the question of this place. You know it's doing Jake no good at all. If you don't know, have a good look at him, next time you've a moment to spare. The question is whether you're going to give it up and go somewhere else.'

I had expected Elizabeth to break in long before this, but even now, when Stella stopped, she said nothing for quite a long time. It was so long that I began to wonder whether physical action had replaced verbal argument, and I ought to go in to prevent serious violence. I was in fact on the point of moving back to the gate when I heard the last sound I expected to hear at that point. Elizabeth was laughing. It was not hysterical laughter. On the contrary, it had a strong dash of theatricality about it. It was calculated and full of malice. Against all previous form, Elizabeth was in control of herself and, at least apparently, of the situation. When she had stopped laughing she said, 'All right, my little spotted spinster, that's torn it right up in little pieces, hasn't it? You know that, don't you? I'm not having you here any more after this. And if you think that's not for me to decide, you're quite, quite wrong, my sweet. I'll decide it all right. I have decided. Nothing dramatic. I'm not turning you out bag and baggage this evening. But you can find some excuse to take yourself off tomorrow and then after a decent interval you can come back once more and collect your stuff. But not any more after that. Never in any circumstances. And if you try to swing Jake on this one, you know what's liable to happen, don't you? Oh no. You're going right out of our lives, little sister. You know it now you've done it, don't you? Now get out of my way. I've got things to do.'

There was nothing after that, nothing more said, no sound at all. The wind went on worrying at the corners of the house, and the sea pounded on the beach, and sucked the pebbles back, and pounded down again as it had done all day and God knows how many days before that. But inside the house no one said anything or seemed to move at all. I walked back round the skirting wall and in at the gate. I was half-way up the path when Stella came out of the side door into the hall and turned out of the open front door to meet me. She walked quite slowly. She had a book in her hand. It still had its jacket on, and I remember thinking I had not seen it before and she must have brought it down from London with her. She looked at me in a curious, calculating way, as if she was meeting me for the first time. She said, 'Hullo, Jake. Been in the wood?'

I nodded. 'Our Dennis was there,' I said. 'He had some chaps with him. I kept out of their way and couldn't see what they were up to. I hope he's not up to anything. I don't trust that man a yard.'

'You can't get hold of it yourself?'

'No. I tried. He won't sell.'

She walked right past me and stood just inside the gate, staring reflectively across at the dark mass of the wood, which in this wind moved, altogether, so little and yet was never still. She said over her shoulder, 'It mightn't be a bad thing if he cut it down. Shall I suggest it to him?'

I said, 'Not if you don't want a murder on your hands.'

She nodded, and walked, still quite slowly, out of the gate and right-handed in the direction of the beach. I went on up the path and into the house. There was no one in the sitting-room on my right. I wondered where Elizabeth was, and then heard her doing things in the kitchen. She was moving about briskly. It sounded as if she was getting supper ready. I put my head round the door and looked in. She did not see me at first. She looked very cheerful and was humming to herself, very quietly. When she saw me she said, 'Hullo, Jake.' As with other things of no particular significance, it sounded exactly like Stella.

I said, 'Our Dennis was in the wood again just now.'

'Doing what?'

'I don't know. I didn't see him to speak to. He had someone with him, I think.'

'Jake, he's not going to do anything awful, is he?'

'I don't know what he's going to do. You can't tell with a man like that. I don't see why it need be anything awful. There's plenty needs doing, God knows.' She shook her head. 'I've got to see this man,' she said. 'I think I'll go over tomorrow and pay a return visit to Mrs Wainwright. Perhaps I'll see him, if he's on show.'

'Try it by all means. But I shouldn't stick your neck out on the subject of the wood. We'll have to wait and see.'

'All right. But I think I'll go, all the same.' She went across the kitchen, opened the refrigerator and peered inside. She said, 'Did you see Stella?'

'Just now? Yes, she was going out as I came in. I think she went down to the beach.'

She nodded and shut the refrigerator with a snap. She was still smiling. I took my head out of the door and shut it quietly after me.

CHAPTER NINE

I never found Carol again in the wood that day. I went to bed in a state of restless misery, partly from simply missing her and partly because I did not like the way Dennis Wainwright had looked at me or the look that came over Carol's face when he was mentioned. Elizabeth left me in peace over her row with Stella, but I did not really like that either. It was against all precedent, and I could not understand it. Stella herself was as silent and unobtrusive as usual and Elizabeth remained very cheerful. The whole evening had a brooding quality that sent me to bed early with nothing to do but listen to the sea on the beach and very little hope of sleep before the early hours of the morning.

I woke late and tired, and was conscious at once that something had changed. It took me some time to realise what it was. The wind had stopped. It must in fact have stopped early in the night, because by morning the sea had lost its menace. No sea on a pebble beach is ever completely silent, but we were back to the Mediterranean murmur that had lulled us during our now unbelievably remote St Luke's summer. Only there was no more summer of any sort. The sky was overcast and the motionless air damp and chilly. We went about almost on tiptoe and talked quietly, uneasy in the unaccustomed silence. Over breakfast Stella said she had remembered an engagement in town and had to get back at once. I went up to my room after breakfast, and when I came down she was gone. Whether she and Elizabeth had had anything more to say to each other I did not know. She did not say good-bye to me.

Elizabeth was pottering in the front of the house. She said, 'That was a very flying visit.'

I said, 'Yes,' refusing to be drawn. She still looked like a cat that has had a good night among the mice, and I did not want to encourage her. I said, 'Are you really going over to the Wainwrights' this morning?'

'I think so. Are you coming?'

'No, no. You do a girl-to-girl drop in on Mrs Wainwright. I have no wish for a heart-to-heart with Dennis. But I'll be interested to hear whether you see him and what you make of him if you do.'

'I'll ask to be introduced,' she said. 'It's time I laid this bogy.'

'Good luck to you,' I said. 'Only don't come back telling me he's charming. I shan't be very easily persuaded.'

'All right, I won't. But I expect he will be, all the same.'

She went off, walking along the beach, when the breakfast things were out of the way. I took the car and set off for Burtonbridge. Half-way along the wood there was a van parked at the side of the track. The back doors were open and a man had his head inside, sorting out some gear I could not see. The van said Barrett & Son, Forestry Contractors. I pulled up short and got out. I walked over and stood behind him, but he still had his head stuck in the van and did not know I was there.

I said, 'You got a job on here?' He stopped doing whatever it was he was doing with his hands and for a second or two hung fire completely, as if he was trying to decide whether he had really heard anything or not. Then curiosity got the better of inertia, and he slowly withdrew himself from inside the van. He turned his head gradually in my direction as he did so, but did not fully straighten up, so that he finished in a curious sort of sideways bow, looking up at me half over his shoulder. He did not say anything, but stayed there looking at me, waiting for me to repeat my question. He was an ageless sort of chap, but I suppose somewhere on the wrong side of forty.

I said, 'Is Mr Barrett doing a job in this wood?' This was pushing things a bit, but I did not think he was the boss, and in my experience country firms do not generally, like solicitors or chartered accountants, take their names from a couple of generations back.

He said, 'Mr. Barrett?' This gave me a moment of misgiving, but he was slowly straightening himself all the time, and the nearer he got to the vertical, the easier I found him to talk to. I nodded encouragingly. 'That's right,' I said. 'You're from Barrett's, aren't you?'

He looked at the side of the van as if he had always wondered what the lettering meant. Then he looked back to me. 'Mr Barrett?' he said. 'He was out here yesterday talking to the gentleman that owns it.'

I nodded again. 'Yes,' I said. 'I saw him, I think. What is Mr Wainwright having done, do you know?'

His eyes wandered again, but before he could say 'Mr Wainwright?' I said, 'The gentleman that owns it.' I jerked my head comprehensively in the direction of the wood and the red brick villa. 'What job does the owner want Mr Barrett to do here?'

He was starting to sink again slowly, as if he longed to take refuge inside the van, but did not want to make too much of a thing of it. In my determination to keep in touch I found myself sinking slowly with him. He saw this and gave up the attempt, and for a moment or two we stayed there, both slightly crouched, gazing at each other between the open rear doors of the van.

Finally he said, 'Clearance job, I reckon. Some sort. You could ask him, of course.'

'Scrub clearance or felling?' I asked. 'Or thinning, perhaps?' I felt the easing of my back muscles before I realised that he had begun to straighten up again. We were almost back to the vertical when he said, 'Felling, too, I reckon. He's over to Burtonbridge, at the office. You could ask him, if you're interested.'

I did not ask him where the office was. I had the name and there is always the local telephone directory. He was sinking again rapidly, but this time I did not follow him down. I said, 'Yes, I'll do that. Thank you.' I felt hollow and slightly sick. I knew the holm oaks needed professional attention, and there was clearance certainly, and probably some thinning, to be done. But I remembered Dennis Wainwright's expression when he said he had his plans for the wood, and I know too much about people like Barrett & Son, with their baby bulldozers and horrible buzz-saws. It was always easy enough to undo the splendour of two centuries, even when a man had to sweat with an axe at the act of destruction. Nowadays it was mechanized mass-slaughter, as much like the axe as the gas-chambers of the genocide are like honest sword and dagger. I had never yet killed anyone for the sake of a tree, but I did not disguise from myself my conviction that a well-grown hardwood is worth any three of the average run of people. If Dennis Wainwright really intended the destruction of the oaks, I would knock him over the head for that alone, apart from my other overriding interest in his death, without hesitation or compunction if I thought I could get away with it.

But I did not know yet that he did. I was full of crawling apprehension, but I did not know for certain. I got back into the car and drove hard for Burtonbridge. I stopped under a No Parking notice and dived into a telephone box. Barrett & Son were in Castle Street. I found a tall young policeman leaning over the car. I said, 'It's not been there half a minute. Tell me where Castle Street is, and I'll take it away at once.'

He straightened up and looked down at me with as much disapproval as he had previously shown of the car. He said, 'Well, sir, it does say No Parking, doesn't it?'

'I know,' I said, 'and I'm really very sorry, but I had to find an address urgently, and I'm a stranger here, pretty well.'

'Who is it you're wanting then, sir, so urgently?'

It was really no business of his, and I could not explain to this nice young country copper, with any hope of being understood, that I was on the trail of a firm of professional mass-murderers. I said, 'A firm called Barrett. It's at 15 Castle Street. If you'll just tell me where that is, I'll never park in the wrong place again as long as I live.'

He decided I was an eccentric, but not dangerous enough to concern him professionally. It was not a bad judgment, though at the moment it erred on the side of leniency. He said, 'All right, sir. We won't say anything more about it now. But you'll have to be more careful in future. It's a bad street, this. If you go down to the bottom and turn left at the lights, you'll be in Fore Street, and second left out of that is Castle Street. But you won't find it easy to leave her there either. You want to go to a proper park really.'

'All right,' I said, 'I will. Thank you very much.' I drove off in an elaborate flurry of unaccustomed hand-signals as if I was trying to pass a test, as in some sense I felt I was. There was, in fact, a gap in the ranks right opposite 15 Castle Street. I left the car there and addressed myself to the doorway. It said Barrett & Son, Forestry Contractors, First Floor. I went up and tapped at a door. A voice said, 'Come in.' It was a local voice, but sharpish. This would be the younger Barrett. His father had probably wielded an axe as somebody's forester in the days when people had forests. The son was a businessman, fully mechanized and interested in results in less than a hundred years. He looked up at me from an old-fashioned desk fairly heavily covered with papers. He had not yet acquired a secretary and an office routine. The face was red and very slightly peevish.

I said, 'Mr Barrett?' and he nodded. 'My name's Haddon,' I said. 'I live out at Marlock, at the Holt House. My uncle had the house for years. Same name.' He nodded again and waited for me to go on. He had sensed, as his kind are very quick to sense, that I had come to ask a favour, and he was stiffening mentally all the time he listened. 'I understand you're doing a job for Mr Wainwright, at Holm Oaks,' I said. 'I saw your man there and he suggested I should come and speak to you.'

He said, 'Yes, Mr Haddon. What is it you want, then?'

'I wondered if you could tell me what it is you're doing for Mr Wainwright? I'm interested in forestry myself, and of course the wood's straight in front of my house. It used to be my uncle's, in fact. He sold it to Mr Wainwright before he died.'

He said, 'You hadn't thought to ask Mr Wainwright?'

'I could, of course. But I was on the way into Burtonbridge when I saw your man. He didn't know the details, but suggested I see you, so I came straight on. Of course, if it's anything confidential—'

He did not like this. He had probably had brushes with the authorities before, and any suggestion of working on the sly had to be rejected. He said, 'Nothing specially confidential. But as we shall be working on Mr Wainwright's instructions—'

I said, 'Look, Mr Barrett. You'll be working straight in front of my house, and I have a right-of-way through the middle of the wood. If I'm sufficiently interested, I can watch the whole job. All I'm asking you is what the job is. I can't see it does any harm for me to know in advance what's going to be done, and my interest is natural enough. But if you'd rather—'

He tried to work out the implications, failed and decided it was safer to be friendly. 'No, that's all right, Mr Haddon. Mr Wainwright's not given us to understand his instructions were in any way confidential. He wants the wood cleared, in fact.'

Something very large and cold settled suddenly in the pit of my stomach, but I pretended not to notice it. 'You mean scrub-clearance and thinning?' I said.

'Not thinning, no. The whole wood's to be cut and the ground cleared.'

I nodded in a matter-of-fact sort of way. 'I see,' I said. 'Any talk of re-planting?'

'Nothing's been said to us. As a matter of fact, I got the impression Mr Wainwright has other uses for the land. But I can't say for certain.'

I nodded briskly. 'I see,' I said. 'All right, thank you, Mr Barrett.' I turned to the door but stopped and turned round again. 'Any idea when you'll be starting on the job?' I said.

'As soon as we can,' he said, 'but it can't be this week, nor the next. I'd say the week after, if we're clear of our other jobs.'

I nodded again. 'Right,' I said. I thanked him and got down to the car. It was not, after all, the Barrett I had to deal with, much as I disliked them and what they stood for. If I had left father and son dead at 15 Castle Street, there would be other mechanized tradesmen ready to do what they were ready to do. It was Dennis Wainwright I had to deal with. It was his decision and they were, God help us all, his trees. I believed more and more in the deliberate malice of my Uncle Clarence. I believed that he had left me the house to spite his proper heirs, and then sold Dennis Wainwright the wood to ensure that I got no blessing with my portion of pottage. If I had never seen the place, the appalling thing Dennis Wainwright was going to do would have happened anyhow, but I should have gone unscathed by it. Now I was directly involved with every threatened tree, and I was tortured by my apparent helplessness to save it.

I drove straight out again on to the Marlock road. When I was clear of the town, I pulled in to the kerb and sat and tried to think the thing out. The trouble was that, apart from a strong superficial repugnance, I knew so little of the man I had to deal with. I had seen next to nothing of him, and by Carol's account inscrutability, even at close range, was his most obvious quality. I did not know why he wanted to cut the wood down, much less how he could be persuaded not to. If it was money he was after—if, for instance, he had discovered some enormously profitable use for the land now under the trees — he could presumably be bought off. But he had not even bothered to enquire my offer when I had suggested buying the wood back from him, and I could not seriously believe that any offer at all within my scope would make him change his mind. Moreover, I did not for a moment really believe that money was his main object. Like my Uncle Clarence, he was out to hurt somebody, or at least to indulge his sense of power over them. I could well believe what Carol had said about the two men's seeing a lot of each other. They would have made a splendid pair. I hoped Uncle Clarence was roasting in hell-fire, and I wished with all my heart that Dennis Wainwright could join him. In the meantime, I wondered whether there was any influence that could be brought to bear, but I had little real doubt that he would resist anything short of compulsion as obstinately as he would resist appeals to his greed.

I had already told myself that I would kill Dennis Wainwright without compunction to save the wood; but now that the practical issue faced me, I doubted, not my resolution, but my ability to commit a successful murder, especially with a victim as formidable as this one. I sat in the car chewing at the thing in a sort of desperate misery; and all the time there lurked in the back of my mind the fear that it might be a knowledge, or at least suspicion, of my meetings with Carol in the wood that had decided her husband to get rid of it. Our meetings there made valuable beyond calculation a thing I should in any case have done murder to preserve; and my love for Carol turned into an almost intolerable hatred the outrage and anger I should in any case have felt at his decision.

I got cold sitting there. The clouds were moving again, and a cold air filtered through the chinks in the car's defences. Finally I started the engine and drove hard for Marlock. The wind freshened all the way, and when I turned eastwards along the northern edge of the wood, it was buffeting the windscreen with considerable force. I stopped in front of the house and with the silencing of the engine heard, filling all the moving air round me, the throb and roar of the sea breaking on the beach. Elizabeth came out of the front door. She saw the car and me sitting there. For a moment she hesitated, then she came running down the flagged path and out of the gate. She snatched at the handle and yanked the door open. 'Jake,' she said, 'oh Jake, something awful's happened.'

CHAPTER TEN

'I know,' I said. 'You don't have to tell me. At least, I suppose we're talking about the same thing. You haven't by any chance murdered our Dennis?'

She shook her head. 'I wish I could. He's going to cut the wood down. Jake, we must stop him.'

'How did you know?'

'Mrs Wainwright told me. He'd said something to her, apparently, that could only mean that. She's as upset as I am, but she can't do anything. She asked me to let you know in case there was anything you could do.'

'I've been talking to the contractors. We've got about ten days. Did you see Dennis himself?'

'No. I don't know where he was. But I didn't want to see him after that.'

'I think I'll have to go over. I don't for a moment imagine I can do much with him, but if I can find out why he's doing it, it might help. It's such a crazy thing to do. You didn't gather anything from Mrs Wainwright?'

We were walking together up the paved path, but now she stopped and turned to me. She said, 'No, but there's something funny going on. I don't know. I got the impression that this business of the wood is a tremendous personal issue between them, but I'm not sure how. But I think she's frightened of him, Jake. She didn't say much, and I haven't even seen him. But if you told me he was doing it just to spite her, I don't think I'd be awfully surprised. I find it all a bit frightening, to be honest.'

We walked up the path, my wife and I, arm in arm and moved by a single thought, thrown for a second time into a sort of spurious intimacy by a common concern for some trees which we valued for different reasons and a woman she did not know I loved. When we got to the house, she said, 'Better have some lunch first. You'll fight better if you're fed. I'll get something quickly.'

'I don't think it's a fight I've got on my hands. He's got the whip hand, after all. All I can do is to appeal to his better feelings, and I don't suppose for a moment he's got any. But mainly it's exploratory. I must penetrate that smooth black shell and see what makes him tick. If I can only find out why he's doing it, we might think of some counter-move that would at any rate stall him off a bit. If he's got a reason, the thing is at least arguable. It's wanton destruction that's so difficult to deal with.'

I ate with very little stomach the cold meal Elizabeth put out for me. Then I walked out of the gate and into the wood. The wind buffeted me in the open ground between. The trees at the western edge leant over and lashed their tops about more than I had ever seen them, but the wood itself stood solid and unmoved, and before I was thirty yards inside it the wind was a noise in the leaves above me, and the roar of the sea had been drowned by the noise of the wind in the leaves. It was very dark. I hurried along the path, obsessed with the secrecy and separateness of the world under the trees, even though today it held no promise for me. I thought of the younger Barrett, with his red face and his machinery, bringing in the daylight and the incessant voice of the sea, and found the thought intolerable.

There was no one about on the road or in the garden of the red house. I went up the steps and pressed a bell-push by the side of the door. I do not know what I expected to happen. The whole place and occasion seemed irretrievably unreal. Carol came to the door, and I said, 'Good afternoon, Mrs Wainwright. Is your husband at home?' It was not only a matter of looking like strangers. We were strangers, unrecognisable to each other in the harsh light of an alien reality.

She said, 'I think he's in the study. Will you come in?'

I followed her through the hall and along a passage. We did not touch or have a word of comfort for each other. She knocked on a shut door, opened it and said, without putting her head in, 'Mr Haddon's here.' Then she stood back and I went in.

Of all things in the world, the first thing I thought of was to wonder what this great bony man was doing in here all by himself. There was nothing to do anything with. The room was as dark and neat and uncommunicative as he was. If he had any personal possessions, he did not leave them about. If he had hobbies or occupations, the gear he worked with was all put away. It was as impersonal as the old-fashioned dentist's waiting-room and had something of the same smell. The second thing I remember was a small shock of surprise, almost, in a perverse way, of disappointment, that this bogy we had built up was so ordinary. He was coiled down in a hard upright chair facing an empty desk. His height, which made him formidable on his feet, went against him like this. He was very slightly ridiculous. He might even have been pathetic, but before I could think so, he smiled, and all my revulsion came back. He did not say anything, but I had not thought he would.

I said, 'Good afternoon, Mr Wainwright. I came to see you because I understand you are proposing to cut down the wood. It may not be true, of course, but I thought I'd like to know one way or the other.'

His expression did not change at all. He was still smiling, but very slightly. He said, 'Who told you this, Mr Haddon?'

'Your contractor, or rather his man. I saw him in his van along the side of the wood. As he was on my private road, I naturally asked him what he was doing.'

'And he told you they were going to cut down the wood?'

'Strictly speaking, he referred me to Mr Barrett, and Mr Barrett told me.'

'Where did you see Mr Barrett?'

'In Burtonbridge, at his office.'

'You went into Burtonbridge specially to make this enquiry? It did not occur to you to come here?'

'In fact, I was on my way into Burtonbridge when I saw the man. At his suggestion I called on Mr Barrett when I got there. This was this morning. I have come to see you as soon as I got home.'

All this time I was standing. There was one other chair in the room. It would have been described in the catalogue as an easy chair, but that was as far as the thing went. It was of dark varnished wood with grained imitation leather upholstery that looked as repellent physically as it was aesthetically. The chair was heavy and away in a far corner. If Mr Wainwright took his ease in it, he must take it where he found it. He did not invite me to do so, nor in fact had I much inclination that way. I stood there in front of his desk, looking down at him coiled in his upright chair. There was no moral advantage in it either way.

He said, 'Well, Mr Haddon, what do you want me to say?' He was still smiling that small slightly uneasy smile, as though I had surprised him in some mildly embarrassing occupation, which he nevertheless enjoyed and insisted on pursuing.

'I want you to tell me the real position,' I said. 'What I should like you to say, of course, is that you have no intention of interfering with the wood at all. But if you have, I naturally want to know what your intentions are.'

He lowered his head at that and looked at me under his rather tufted brows and bony forehead. He said, 'Interfere? What do you mean, interfere? It's my wood, isn't it? The interference is not on my side, Mr Haddon.'

I forgot my repugnance in my desperate need to establish some communication with him. I put my hands on the front of his empty desk and leant forward, so that my face was within a yard of his. 'But the wood is there in its own right,' I said. 'It was there before you were here. It will be there after you are dead, if you will only leave it alone. It is alive itself and has a right to go on living. You can't cut down a tree, let alone a whole wood, as if you were knocking down a breeze-block garage.'

I knew as I said it that this was all wrong. I had not meant to declare my interest in this way, or certainly not to start with. It is no good opening negotiations with a declaration of irreconcilable fundamentals. He shook his head in very nearly honest bewilderment.

'The wood is mine,' he said again. 'I bought it from your uncle before I even knew you existed. It is solely for me to decide what to do with it.'

He had stopped smiling now. His eyes, grey and enormous and wide open, stared up into mine and his mouth was very slightly open.

'But why?' I said. 'Why did you buy it? You paid a very full price for it. I don't know what your contract with Barretts' is, but you won't see your money back this way. Even as a straight matter of business, it would pay you to work on the wood before you sell anything. Or did you buy it simply in order to destroy it?'

He made a slight, unattractive sound in his throat, as if he was trying to swallow with his mouth open. He did not say anything, but shook his head very slowly from side to side. He did not take his eyes off mine. I said, 'Why do you want to destroy it? What good is it going to do you? I can't understand. Have you any other use for the land?'

He went on shaking his head slowly. It did not express any particular negative so much as the fundamental variance of our points of view. He said, 'You didn't know your uncle at all well, I think, Mr Haddon?'

'I didn't know him at all.'

'No. Well. I knew him fairly well. He had no great love for the wood, I think.'

'Or for anything else, by all accounts.'

'No? That's a possible view, I suppose. But he wouldn't part with the wood until he knew he was dying. By then he knew me well enough to let me have it.'

'But why did you buy it?'

He put his hands on the table, only a very little distance from mine. They were large white square hands, but as neutral as the rest of him. He began to get up. 'I bought it because it was there, Mr Haddon. I could not leave it there, not like that, in anyone else's hands. I am destroying it for the same reason – because it is there. I am not interested in the financial aspects of the thing at all. So there is really nothing you can do. Perhaps if you had never come—'

He was looking down at me now. I said, 'If I were to go away, leave the Holt House altogether—'

He shook his head decisively at that. 'It's too late,' he said. 'Much too late in the day. Whatever you did now, I should not leave a tree standing. I cannot have it there any longer.'

I saw his eyes turn towards the door before I heard, at any rate consciously, what made him do it. There was an impatient tap-tap of a woman's heels in the hall and someone put a hand on the door handle. I looked back at Dennis Wainwright and saw him for a moment, half in profile, as he stared at the door. His whole face was clotted with speechless fury. It was quite pale, but the eyes protruded and the underlip jutted savagely. Then he flicked his eyes sideways at me, and for a moment longer we stared at each other, both in our opposite ways obsessed with the person we expected and both almost clinically interested in each other's obsession. We were still looking at each other when the door opened and Elizabeth came in.

It is the standard comment, but would not be strictly true, to say that I do not know which of us was the more surprised. As a matter of fact, I know quite well. He was. I at least knew who Elizabeth was, and although this move on her part was certainly unexpected, it did not take me very long to see it as at least partly in character. Dennis Wainwright had never seen Elizabeth at all. He had to get over the shock of the extreme physical divergence from what he expected and then make up his mind who she was. It was all a matter of split seconds, of course. But for an almost measurable time he was completely at a loss.

She hardly looked at me. She walked straight up to him and stood facing him, on his side of the desk. She meant to look, and succeeded in looking, extremely appealing. She said: 'Mr Wainwright? Mr Wainwright, won't you please reconsider your decision about the wood? Couldn't you at least postpone it? It means so much to me.'

He looked down at her upturned face for quite a while before he half turned to me. He said, 'Your wife, Mr Haddon?' Then his eyes went back to Elizabeth, and quite suddenly he grinned. It was totally unexpected and rather horrifying. I had only seen him smile his small smile before, but when he uncovered his teeth like this, they were the darkest part of his face. All the rest was grey and white, but the teeth were large, regular, shining and quite a dark yellow. The pair of them made a remarkable picture, there on the far side of the empty desk. Elizabeth, as I have already had occasion to say, could still pass for a beautiful woman, and was all pink and gold. The odd thing was that, for all he gave me the horrors, Dennis Wainwright, when he was on his feet, was an impressive looking creature. I knew for an absolute certainty that Elizabeth was doing this deliberately, but I could see the waves passing between them, and I knew that Elizabeth would tell me afterwards, despite my warning, that he was rather charming. Meanwhile he grinned at her and said, 'I had not expected to find you among the wood's defenders, Mrs Haddon. My wife is a regular devotee, and so, I believe, is your husband. I had not somehow imagined—'

'It's the birds, Mr Wainwright. That is my great interest. You have some very rare species there. One at least that has not been observed in this part of the country for quite a time. If you could at least give me time to complete my observations, that would be something saved at any rate. Can't I persuade you?'

He shook his head at her. He was smiling his more ordinary smile now. He was completely oblivious of my presence, and I had a sudden, certain conviction that he enjoyed shaking his head at Elizabeth much more than he enjoyed shaking it at me.

'Bird-watching?' he said. 'I had not imagined the wood's attractions were so various. No, Mrs Haddon. I have just told your husband that no decision on his part could make me change my mind. I will not have the wood there any longer. The birds can go elsewhere. They cannot, certainly, be breeding any longer.' He half grinned at her again. 'I know something about the local birds myself,' he said. 'I knew we had our rarities, though I must confess I did not know of anything as compelling as you suggest. But I'm afraid that must take its chance along with the rest.'

Elizabeth no longer had her head tilted back. She had drawn in her chin while he was speaking and was looking at him now fixedly from under her eyebrows. I wondered where I had seen that fixed, deadly stare before, and remembered that it was a trick of Stella's I had not up to then observed in Elizabeth. I knew she was blindingly angry, and I did not, on previous experience, think it best for her to vent her anger here. I walked across to the door and opened it. Unexpectedly, Elizabeth seemed perfectly aware of what I had done. She turned her back on Dennis Wainwright and went out of the room. She did not stamp out, but went with a curiously deliberate, almost mincing gait, as if she was conscious at each step what she was putting her foot on.

I nodded, 'I'm sorry to have taken up your time, Mr Wainwright,' I said, and he nodded back. His eyes had followed Elizabeth out of the door, and we both heard the front door shut before either of us moved.

CHAPTER ELEVEN

I do not think, looking back, that I ever spoke to Dennis Wainwright again, except on one occasion. I certainly had no further direct contact with him during the next few days, despite the fact that they were almost wholly occupied with an intensive struggle to defeat his purpose and save the oak wood. But it was all done at second-hand, as we brought our heavy guns to bear, one after the other, on the enemy position. I knew his side of it only so far as I could get it from Carol.

I went out of the house leaving him in his dark, stale-smelling study, and saw nobody anywhere. Elizabeth must have left almost at the run, and probably went home along the beach. I know she did not go through the wood, and if she had taken the track on the north side, she would still have been on the road when I left the Wainwrights' gate. I myself went as I had come, through the wood, and found Carol waiting for me at a turn of the path.

I said, 'Did you see Elizabeth?'

'Elizabeth? No. Was she there?'

'She came a few minutes after me. She came straight to the study. I wondered whether you had shown her in.'

She shook her head. 'I came out here as soon as you went in. But I think she knows where the study is – I think I told her this morning. And she would have heard your voices from the hall. What happened, Jake?'

'Nothing. I asked him politely and Elizabeth asked him pathetically. I pleaded for the trees and she pleaded for the birds. He said he didn't mind where the birds went. He wanted the trees down and didn't care about the money or anything else. That was when I pointed out that he'd lose money by cutting now.'

'It's not true, you know. Money is almost incredibly important to him. I think it's true that he's prepared to face a loss, on balance, over the wood, but if somebody offered him an enormous sum to save the trees, or threatened him with enormous penalties if he cut them down, I don't believe for a moment that he'd go on with it.'

'I can't offer him an enormous sum, unfortunately. In any case, it would have to be phenomenally large before he accepted it from me. I don't know about penalties. That's one of the things I've got to look into, if we're going to go on fighting the thing. But there's so little time.'

We had been walking slowly along the path with our eyes mostly on the ground. I think we were holding hands. But now I stopped and swung her round to face me. I said, 'Carol, let's not fight it. It's nothing compared with the main issue. Will you leave your husband and come with me? Elizabeth can have the house. Perhaps if we're gone, he won't be so bent on destroying the wood. Carol, beloved, will you come? I don't see what else we can do. Trees or no trees, we can't go on as we are.'

For a moment she leant against me. Her face was turned down and I could see only the top of her dark head. I believed I could feel the throb of the veins in her temples as she rested her head against me, but it must really have been my own heart. As soon as she looked up I knew it was no use. Her face was immensely grave, and she was full of the in-turned, withdrawn quality I had seen so much of when I first knew her. Whatever kind of a hell she was in, it was her private hell. She did not expect me to pull her out of it, and made no pretence of being able to do much for me so long as she was in it. She said, 'We can't go on as we are.'

This was an entirely new statement. The fact that I had myself just used the same words meant nothing at all. Whether or not she had heard me say them, she now spoke out of her private hell with an authority which I could not question, but which chilled me to the heart. 'And I can't go away with you because of Elizabeth. I think you know that yourself.'

I said, 'But you don't like Elizabeth.' I knew it was foolish as I said it, but I did not expect the violence with which she threw it back at me.

'Of course I don't like her. But we can't get away from her. If she were to leave you, it would be all right. But she's not going to, not Elizabeth. She's perfectly happy as she is, and she'd be very unhappy without you. Particularly if you'd gone off with the brunette next door. Therefore you can't get away from her, Jake my dear, not you. And if you can't, we can't. I'm not going to compete with a mournful Elizabeth at the other end of the pillow. And as it's that or nothing, it will have to be nothing, won't it?'

She pushed herself away from me to arms' length, and for a long time we looked at each other as if we had never seen each other before. In a sense I believe we never had. She was exercising to the full the woman's dreadful ability to make a man feel young, ignorant and irresponsible in these matters. I do not for a moment believe that she wanted, consciously, to make me feel young, ignorant and irresponsible but she was full of the vast female gravity before which the man's sick heartache takes on the temporary tolerability of indigestion and seems almost equally undignified. I have never known, and probably never shall know, whether a woman really gets hurt more than a man. I find it, in my more cautious moments, difficult to reconcile with that superior nervous toughness which keeps her going, time and again, when the weaker vessel cracks. But there is no doubting her conviction of deeper suffering or her ability to communicate it, at any rate temporarily, to her partner.

She looked at me, this woman I loved so much, out of the appalling unplumbed depths of female unhappiness, and I stood before her, almost unable to meet her eye, a self-convicted philanderer. I said, 'Don't do this all at once. Don't meet me for a bit, if it's better not. But don't shut the door all at once. Give me time to think, at least.'

She said, 'Oh Jake, Jake.' She pulled me to her again, but would not kiss me. Then she turned and ran off through the wood. I went along the path, under the dark threshing trees, while the hard fact of an immeasurable, comfortless future slowly permeated my mind. I stopped, half turned round and went on again. I said, 'You can't, Carol, you can't,' aloud. But I did not for a moment believe she could not.

When I got to the house, the car was gone and so was Elizabeth. I went into the empty kitchen and began to put on a kettle, mechanically, because it seemed the right thing to do at that time of day. Then I thought better of it and turned it off. I do not know how long it was before I heard the car coming back and went out to meet her. She must have left the car door open. I did not hear her shut it, and usually she slammed it fit to have the hinges off. She came running up the path towards me. Her whole face was aflame with excitement. She said, 'Jake,

I think we can stop him. I've been into Burtonbridge. But you've got to help me. You will, won't you?'

I said, 'Of course I'll help you,' not minding, at that moment, whether they cut down all the oaks in England. 'I've just put on a kettle. Let's have some tea and then tell me what's to be done.'

She nodded and went straight through into the kitchen. I sat till she brought the tray, trying to convince myself of a world in which a call to action had any validity. I suppose she found that the kettle was not on and relit it, but she did not say anything. She knew something was up. She put the tray down, poured me out a cup, handed it to me and for a long covert moment looked at me. Then she said, 'I've been to the County Council. I couldn't see the man I wanted. One never can. But there was a good girl at Enquiries. They can issue a Tree Preservation Order, or something of the sort. Only we've got to move fast. It's no good today. Will you come in tomorrow morning?'

'All right. Do you know the man you want?'

'A man called Absolam. But I expect he's all right.'

'He ought to be interested in oaks, anyway.' My small joke took me by surprise, like a voice from a world I thought no longer existed. Elizabeth passed it over altogether. 'If I were you,' I said, 'I'd ring up first thing in the morning and make an appointment to see this Absolam. Otherwise he'll be in committee or drinking coffee. He's an official, I imagine, not a member?'

'Oh, I think so. I mean part of the office staff.'

'Good. Start with him, by all means. We'll probably have to chase the local legislators later, but let's get the facts from an official first.'

I walked along the beach in the evening, going westwards into the wind and away from the wood. The sea bellowed on the stones at my left hand. The place would take some living in even if Carol had never existed. With her present but unavailable at the far end of the wood, it was immediately and demonstrably intolerable. I turned and came back with the wind behind me, moving quietly into a lethargy of despair. For the first time in what felt like weeks, I fell asleep as soon as I was in bed and slept through in one piece. This was no doubt nature applying balm to my hurt mind, but it did not, on balance, do me much good. I woke up unable to accept the reality I had grappled with the night before, and had to absorb it gradually all over again as the day took its course, and I had no expectation of seeing Carol on this or any other day.

At breakfast Elizabeth said, 'I rang up but couldn't get a reply. Do you think it will be all right?'

I looked at my watch. It was still not nine. 'Good God,' I said, 'you don't really think there's going to be a girl on the switchboard, let alone Mr Absolam at his desk, by half past eight? Try after breakfast. There'll be someone about then.' We left, in fact, at about half past ten with an appointment to see Mr Absolam at a quarter past eleven. The journey could not possibly take us longer than twenty-five minutes and did not. We parked outside and looked hungrily at the seat of power. It was a new seat of power, built in pre-stressed Georgian among the pleasant surroundings of a rural county town that still had space to spare. It was no good roaming about outside and impolitic to go in before our time. I persuaded Elizabeth to drink coffee while Mr Absolam had his, and we turned up at the Enquiries window a minute before the quarter past.

The girl was, as Elizabeth had said, good. She was a sharp visaged blonde with a quick mind and a husband somewhere in the background. She said, 'Mrs Haddon?' politely and smiled at me over Elizabeth's shoulder. 'Mr Absolam can see you at once. It's about a Tree Preservation Order, isn't it? I've told him. Will you come this way?' We went down the corridors of power. The doors were enamelled pale green and neatly ticketed with names. It had none of the old-world charm of Whitehall. Mr Absolam's room was small and full of plans. Mr Absolam himself was gigantic. He was shaggy, saturnine and educated-local in speech. He waved us to chairs, sat down again at his desk and said, 'Well, now?', rubbing his enormous hands together.

Elizabeth looked at me, but I pretended not to notice. It was her hare. Let her chase it. I only reserved the right to head it if it looked like running completely wild. She said, 'We live at Marlock, in a house called The Holt House right above the beach. There's a wood of holm oaks in front of the house. It stretches along just above the beach. It's quite a big wood.' Mr Absolam raised one shaggy eyebrow. I said, 'Nearly six acres, I'd say,' and he lowered it again. Elizabeth said, 'It's owned by a Mr Wainwright now. It used to go with The Holt House, but the previous owner sold it to Mr Wainwright. He says he's going to cut it down. It would be a crime, Mr Absolam. I-we wondered whether he could be stopped.'

Mr Absolam nodded shaggily and heaved himself up to look at the survey map on the wall behind his desk. 'Marlock?' he said. 'I don't know—Oh yes, I see.' He made a gentle hissing noise in his teeth and then said, 'What does the wood consist of, Mrs Haddon? Holm oaks, you said. Anything else?'

Elizabeth said, 'I don't think—' and looked at me again.

'No,' I said. 'It was clearly a piece of deliberate plantation. And right above the sea like that I suppose they didn't want to try anything else. It needs thinning, but the trees are well-grown now, and generally speaking in very good condition. I'm not an expert, but I'm interested in trees. I shouldn't say there could be any possible case for doing more than a bit of thinning. And the wood adds greatly to the character of the place.'

Mr Absolam nodded. 'Well,' he said, 'he'd want a felling licence to start with. That's a Forestry Commission job. Do you suppose he's got one? Is he aiming to do the cutting himself, do you know?'

'No,' said Elizabeth. 'He's got in a contractor.' She looked at me again.

'Barrett and Son,' I said. 'In Castle Street.'

He nodded again. 'We know them,' he said. 'Well, as I say, first he is got to have a licence to cut more than a few hundred cubic foot of wood. That's under the Forestry Act. Then if we put a Preservation Order on, he can't fell at all. That's a matter of amenity value under the Town and Country Planning Act. This looks a good case, but of course that's for the Committee to decide.'

I thought, 'Now we're coming to it.' I said, 'Which committee in fact?'

'Well, the County Planning Committee makes the Order, subject to confirmation by the Minister.'

'And what moves the County Planning Committee?'

'Well, they'd act on a resolution of the Planning, Reference and General Purposes Committee. That's a Sub-Committee of the Planning Committee, really.'

'And what starts the Sub-Committee resolving?'

'The P.R. and G.P. Committee? Well, they'd have a recommendation from the Tree Preservation Sub-Committee.'

'And how often do they meet?'

'Them? Once a month. As a matter of fact, they had a meeting only three days ago.'

Elizabeth said, 'But—' Mr Absolam shifted his dark face to her for a moment and then came back to me. I said, 'Look, Mr Absolam. Your Tree Preservation Sub-Committee is due to meet in four weeks' time. They recommend to another Committee, and when that meets it issues an Order which the Minister still has to confirm. That looks like Christmas if we're lucky. Wainwright's going to start felling the week after next. Aren't there any emergency procedures?'

'Ah. Soon as all that, is it? Well, we can do a bit in anticipation, if we have to. Get the Order out, and get the Minister to give provisional approval. But we've got to have the recommendation from the Tree Preservation Sub-Committee.'

'And they don't meet for another month.'

'Well, not in the ordinary course, they don't. But they could call an emergency meeting, I expect, if the facts were there. If I were you,' he said, turning suddenly to Elizabeth, 'I'd go and see Mr Greenslade. He's Chairman. He'd know your wood, I expect. It's his interest, you see. He knows most of the woodlands in the county. If he takes your view of the matter, he could get things moving all right. In the meantime, I don't mind having a word with the Forestry Commission and telling them what's going on. And if there's no licence been issued, I expect they'd send someone out to have a word with this Mr Wainwright. Just to tell him the requirements, and so on. And then I don't mind having a word with Jim Barrett. He wouldn't want to have trouble over the job, I'm sure, and if we told him there was a Preservation Order on the way, I expect he'd hold things up a bit. But you want to go and see Mr Greenslade really.'

'We'll go,' I said. 'We'll go now. But I still don't see—Supposing Mr Greenslade is a hundred per cent on our side and sets everything in motion as fast as he can – how long will it be before you can get your Order provisionally confirmed?'

Mr Absolam got up, darkening all the small room. 'I reckon we could do it in a week,' he said.

CHAPTER TWELVE

'I like my Mr Absolam,' said Elizabeth. 'He's shaggy and comforting, like a very big dog. But what a game it is. All those committees, and in fact if you push them the thing can be fixed in a week.'

'Not permanently fixed. All we're asking for is a stand-still order, after all. I've no doubt the Act provides for objections to the Order and appeals to the Minister within thirty days and God knows what else. All we're trying to do is to see that no trees are cut until the law has taken its course. It's like an interim injunction from a civil court. You can get them quick enough if there's a reasonable case and if the whole thing can be made nonsense of if the other side's allowed to do what it wants in the meantime. But it doesn't settle anything permanently.'

Elizabeth said, 'What happens if our damned Dennis says to hell with the Orders; I'm cutting anyhow? He's in a mood to at the moment.'

I stopped short on the synthetic marble floor of the entrance hall. 'Damn,' I said. 'I forgot to ask about that. I think I'll go back and have a word with Mr Absolam. But there's one thing, Absolam's evidently going to put the fear of God into Barretts', and if they drag their feet, Dennis can't do much. If he starts in with his little chopper, it will be an awful long time before he gets far into the wood. Unless he bark-rings them or something. He's capable of it, but probably he wouldn't think of it. Anyway, let me go and have another word with Absolam.'

I put my head round the door. Mr Absolam flashed his teeth at me, but did not speak or get up. 'I forgot to ask about sanctions,' I said. 'What about enforcement? What penalties are involved?'

He pointed to a chair and I sat down. 'That's where we're weak,' he said. 'If we make an Order and the owner goes on felling, all it costs him is a maximum fifty-pound fine with an additional two quid a day for as long as he goes on. Well, it can be ten quid a day later. But look at it – it's pathetic. With modern tools, felling a wood is a matter of a few days, not weeks or months. The Authority says, "Don't cut down those trees," and the owner says, "Thanks, but I think I will. Here's a hundred quid for the privilege of breaking the law." And the felled trees are still his and may be worth a packet. The Act's all right, but there's no teeth in it. What saves us half the time is that people don't know what's involved. They see the Order and think there's no arguing with it. They don't look into it and see what's involved. Lucky for us they don't. This Mr Wainwright of yours – is he likely to be troublesome, do you think?'

'Very troublesome indeed, I should say. Doesn't like parting with money, but bloody-minded about the trees, all right.'

He nodded. 'Well, there's two things. First, he can't do it himself, and I think I can frighten Barretts' off, for a bit, any how. More important, there's the Forestry Act. That's better off for penalties. If he exceeds his felling licence, or fells when a licence has been refused, he can be fined twice the value of the trees cut. Well – if this wood is what you say, that's going to add up to quite a bit. Mind you, it's still no good if the trees aren't worth much and the owner has a profitable use for the land. But in this case, it ought to do, even if Mr Wainwright looks into what's involved. And as I say, most of them don't.'

I nodded and got up. 'Thank you very much,' I said. 'You'll get on to the Forestry Commission, will you? We'll go and see Mr Greenslade.' He nodded and reached for his telephone. 'I will,' he said. I left him to it.

Elizabeth was clacking up and down impatiently on the synthetic marble. She said, 'Well, can they send him to jail?'

'No, unfortunately. But they can fine him twice the value of the wood if he cuts it in defiance of their orders. And that's going to be a pretty tidy sum. I can't see our Dennis risking that, even if he considers defiance at all. He takes his money much too seriously.'

She looked at me, slightly puzzled. 'But he said he didn't care about the money at all. He was having the trees down regardless. Don't you think he means that? I must say, I believed him. Or did he say anything else after I'd gone?'

I shook my head knowingly, while my mind flew round in a small, rapid circle and settled down again. 'No,' I said, 'but I don't see Dennis getting himself stuck in public. He might swallow a private loss to indulge his spite, but being hauled before the courts and fined a packet, virtually on our information, is another thing.'

As we got into the car she said, 'I hope you're right. I don't really see what he's got to be spiteful about. To me, I mean.'

'I'm fairly certain I'm right,' I said. 'Anyway, old Absolam's going to scare off the contractors, for the time at least. I feel myself that the situation is in hand. But let's find this Greenslade.'

Mr Greenslade lived three miles out on the other side of Burtonbridge. After we had gone a mile and a half Elizabeth said, 'She's a funny woman, Mrs Wainwright.' I made an exploratory noise, expecting her to go on, but she never did. When we got to the village, she said, 'There's the house. Leisure, he said. Sounds suburban. Golly, it is, too.' I stopped. It certainly was. It looked almost incredibly out of place in that thatched, embowered countryside, as if some lunatic enthusiast had numbered each pink brick and reverently transported the thing, bit by bit, from its original site in Kenton or Harrow Weald. I had expected Mr Greenslade to be a sort of green man, who would have bark on his knuckles and would need, once a month, not so much a haircut as pruning. This must have been the name and his known interest in woodlands. He could hardly have been more different. He had probably built the house himself because it was the kind of house he liked and was used to. He was smallish and bright pink and point-device in his accoutrements. How long he had been settled here I did not know, but his speech was the terrible speech of the south Midlands. He was sitting in a garden chair of striped canvas over steel tubes. Except for a small laburnum, there was not a tree in sight.

I leant over the gate and said, 'Mr Greenslade, they're going to cut down the Marlock holt.'

He got up slowly and came over to the gate. He said, 'No, not really? The howlm owks? Tst, tst, that's too bad. We can't have that, can we?' He opened the gate. 'Come in, Mr—I don't know your name.' He nodded to Elizabeth, but made no attempt to include her in the conversation. 'Who's the owner now, then? Used to be a chap called Haddon, but there's new people come. Who sent you to me – Absolam?'

'Yes,' I said. 'My name's Haddon, as a matter of fact, but unfortunately I'm not the owner. The previous owner was my uncle. He left me the house but sold the wood before he died. The present owner's a Mr Wainwright, who lives at the eastern end of the holt.'

Elizabeth could not gaze up at Mr Greenslade, but she gazed down at him without losing any of the effect. She said, 'Mr Greenslade, please, you can't let him do it. It would be so wicked. And there's no need. He's only doing it out of spite.' She nicked her eyes sideways at me. 'We none of us want the wood destroyed. Even his wife doesn't want it. Mr Absolam said your Committee could stop it. Only there's very little time.'

'Doing it soon, is he? What about the Forestry Commission? Do they know?'

'Mr Absolam's telling them,' I said. 'As far as we know, there's no licence to fell. But we hoped there might be a Preservation Order as well. It's a cast-iron case, Mr Greenslade, surely?'

He nodded to me and then smiled up at Elizabeth. 'What do you want me to do, then? Get my Sub-Committee to make a recommendation for them to rush through at County Hall?'

Elizabeth said, 'Oh, please, yes.'

I said, 'Mr Absolam told us you might call an emergency meeting when the thing was as urgent as this.'

'Yes, well, that's not difficult. There's only five on the Sub-Committee and three's a quorum. One of our members represents your Division on the Council, as a matter of fact. He'll know the holt. I tell you what. Let me have a word with Absolam and then we'll decide what's to be done. Won't be a minute. Sit down.' He waved a hand vaguely in the direction of the single garden chair and went into the house. We looked at each other across the chair. Elizabeth said, 'A bit late in the year for that, don't you think?' I nodded and we turned to opposite sides of the minute grass plot. The excitement had gone out of the chase, and a wave of the most appalling unhappiness rolled over me. I did not know, after all, why I was doing this, and of all things in the world I could not bear Elizabeth's company. Inside the house I could hear Mr Greenslade calling somebody Miss. If that was the sharp blonde, she would not like it. She was a cut above being called Miss by anyone, apart from the fact that she had a husband and a wedding-ring to prove it. Then he got through to Mr Absolam. I heard a door shut, and pictured him pushing it shut with his heel, looking over his shoulder in our direction. There was no subtlety about Mr Greenslade.

Elizabeth said, 'I wonder how in the world he got on the Council? He can't be a local.'

'Retired man, I should say. But still full of energy and with a particular hobby-horse to ride. He'd get the Tories to take him up and run him. There's not much competition for nomination here, I don't think. We're lucky to have him, on my reckoning.'

'Oh yes. I'm all for Greensleeves. I'm just surprised at him, that's all.'

The door opened and Mr Greenslade was with us again. He was rubbing his hands. 'I've had a word with Absolam,' he said. 'The Forestry are sending a man out tomorrow to have a word with the owner and let him know the requirements of the Forestry Act about licences for felling. Then the Local Authority will get one of their surveyors out there – the Rural District man, probably – to let us have a report on details of acreage, value and the rest. In the meantime, I'm going to get my Sub-Committee together straight away. They can make a recommendation on' – he bowed to Elizabeth – 'Mrs Haddon's information subject to confirmation by the surveyor's report. We can leave the rest to Absolam.'

He stood for a moment warming himself in the golden glow of Elizabeth's approbation. Then he put himself, very deliberately, into an old tweed jacket he had brought out of the house on his arm. 'I wonder,' he said, 'if you could help me by giving me a lift in your car? I don't have one. Ought to, I suppose, really.' He looked at us in mild bewilderment at his own neglect.

'The car is at your disposal,' I said. 'We all are.'

He said, 'That's right,' as if we were children who had made a sensible decision. Elizabeth got into the back and Mr Greenslade came beside me. 'As a matter of fact,' he said, 'when I said hold a meeting, it's more a matter of having a word with a couple of members.' I drove off, seeing in my mind's eye the long epic of Mr Greenslade, as the almost self-appointed champion of the county's trees, having words all over the place with other, lesser champions in the mysterious generation of legal authority. 'If you don't mind going to Seddington first,' he said, 'we'll have a word with Colonel Beecham. Won't take long. Off the main road on the left ahead here. Not more than five miles, it can't be.'

Colonel Beecham had clipped yew hedges, at least two gardeners and hunters in a paddock. The thatch was perfect. The roses were nearly over. The Colonel leant into the car – Mr Greenslade made no attempt to get out – and made his compliments to Elizabeth. He called Mr Greenslade Tom. 'O' course, Tom,' he said, 'o' course. Quite agree. Got to be stopped. Better get Mike Grainger. It's his Division and he'll know it.'

'I was going to,' said Mr Greenslade.

'Good,' said the Colonel. 'Fine. You get hold of Mike and take it as settled.' He asked how long we had been at Marlock, hoped we liked the place, regretted having missed us, hoped he would see us again soon, and waved us off down his perfect gravel between the yew hedges.

'Good old sport,' said Mr Greenslade. 'Does a surprising amount for his age. Now left if you don't mind. Grainger's got a farm at Seele. Not far from you, in fact.'

From behind us Elizabeth said, 'This Mr Grainger – he's our local member of the Council, is he?'

Not being concerned with the road, Mr Greenslade swivelled round and talked over the back of the seat. 'That's right. Quite a young chap, but he farms in a big way. Go-ahead, you know. Got ideas. He won't be left off the bus for want of pushing, Mike Grainger won't. Sees himself in Parliament, I shouldn't wonder. But I don't know.' He paused and swung slowly round in his seat again.

'Not your idea?' I said.

'Well – I've got nothing against him myself. He's a worker and he's got sense. A bit of side doesn't worry me if a man's got something to shout about. But I don't see him ever getting adopted. Not the type the constituencies go for. A bachelor, to start with. Apt to get himself talked about, and in the wrong way. You know.'

Elizabeth, from the back, said, 'The Romeo of the Rural District?'

'County, anyhow,' I said. 'But that's it, is it, Mr Greenslade? One for the girls, rather?'

He nodded, a little gloomily. 'That's what they say,' he said. 'It's none of my business, and he's a good Councillor to my way of thinking. Only if he's going to get any further, he wants to marry and settle down. That's as I see it, anyhow. Left here, Mr Haddon. There's the sign for Seele. You can't miss it now.'

The farm was a bevy of modern buildings, expensive, efficient and quite startlingly ugly. Somewhere in the middle of them, an old stone farmhouse had been modernized without much taste. The farmer had a long-chassis Landrover, a black Jaguar and an enormous range of polychrome farm machinery. The air was full of mechanical voices. At this hour at any rate there was no livestock to be seen. A boy with a smirk I did not like said, 'Mr Grainger? He's in the office.' He looked speculatively at Elizabeth. 'Shall I tell him?' he said.

'Tell him Tom Greenslade wants him on County Council business, will you?' Mr Greenslade clearly did not like the boy either. He sat back in his seat and waited. We all waited for perhaps five minutes. Then Mike Grainger came to us across the yard, stepping delicately. The Romeo of the Rural District he might be, but I did not think for a moment it would stop there. There was much more to him than that. His looks were quite spectacular and his clothes, even at home on a working morning, were far from local. He said, 'Hi there, Tom,' swept the other two of us with a blue appraising eye and bowed gravely to Elizabeth. There was nothing wrong with his manners. Mr Greenslade did not introduce us. He said, 'It's about a Tree Preservation Order, Mike. The holt at Marlock. Do you know it?' Mike Grainger's eyes came round to us again. I thought he nodded very slightly, but mainly to himself.

'I know it,' he said. 'A man called Wainwright owns it now. Queer type, by all accounts. Is he threatening to fell it?'

'Seems so. And he's in a hurry, so we want emergency action. All right?'

'All right by me, Tom. It's a nice bit of wood. And uncommon, as close to the sea as that. How did you hear of it?'

Mr Greenslade put down his forced hand with a flourish. 'Ah,' he said, 'meet Mr and Mrs Haddon. Mr Haddon owns the Holt House. His uncle used to own the wood, but sold it to this Mr Wainwright seemingly. It's Mrs Haddon we're indebted to really. She got on to Absolam at the office and he sent them on to me.'

Mike Grainger did not lean on the side of the car. He kept his distance, smiling beautifully. The smile singed the top of my right shoulder on its way to the back seat. 'How do you do?' he said. 'I should have looked in to see you, but Tom will tell you I'm a desperately busy man.'

Elizabeth said, 'He's already told us.'

'Good. That must be my excuse then. As a matter of fact,' he said to Elizabeth, 'I believe I know your sister.'

CHAPTER THIRTEEN

The thing was unimportant, but I found it slightly surprising. I should not have thought that Mike Grainger was Stella's kind, except that he was so perfect aesthetically. What surprised me more was Elizabeth's reaction. I should not have been surprised if she had been taken aback, or inquisitive, or even, seeing that gorgeous creature standing there, a little jealous. As it was, she said, 'Stella? Yes. I think she said she had met you.' She said it in her grand-duchess voice, with, to my ears, a faint hint of amusement in it. I did not turn round, but I knew she was smiling slightly, and the splendid Mike was certainly smiling back at her.

It was Mr Greenslade who broke up the mutual entertainment. He said, 'Well, Mike. I've already seen the Colonel. I'll tell Absolam to get out the usual minute and give the others a ring. Now if you wouldn't mind getting me back, Mr Haddon? Seems a shame when you're so near home, but it can't be helped.'

'That's all right,' I said. 'It's the least I can do. You wouldn't like to run out to Marlock, I suppose, now that we're almost there, and have a look at the holt yourself? My wife might like to be dropped there, rather than come all the way back.' I turned to Elizabeth, but Mr Greenslade said, 'No, no, thank you, no need. I'd like to get back, as a matter of fact.' Elizabeth stuck her tongue out at the back of his head and I turned to my driving. We took our leave of the farmer in our different styles, and as the car moved off he raised his hand in a comprehensive gesture. It was rather like a high priest of Priapus blessing the departing congregation.

I said over my shoulder, 'Where did Stella meet him?' I could not say more with Mr Greenslade beside me, for all his doubts about Mike Grainger. As it turned out, the grand duchess was in any case still in residence. She said, 'I really don't know. On one of her journeys, perhaps. She just mentioned it.' I nodded and left it at that. I always left everything as it was, so far as I could, in matters lying between Elizabeth and Stella. As so often, I suspected undercurrents here, but was almost desperately concerned to keep my feet out of them. I turned to Mr Greenslade. 'Well, now, Mr Greenslade,' I said, 'what about this meeting of yours?'

'Well,' he said, 'we've had it, really, as near as we need. Grainger and the Colonel and myself constitute a quorum of the Sub-Committee, and we're all agreed. Absolam will do the rest on paper. We shall have met to consider information supplied by Mrs Haddon and confirmed by the surveyor's report – got to get that in first, of course, but he'll allow for that – and we'll have resolved to recommend a Preservation Order. Absolam will tell the other two members. It's all perfectly regular. Well, when I say regular, it's short-circuited a bit, but what's the difference? A majority of the Committee are agreed. The effect's the same in the long run. The rest is just red tape.'

Elizabeth said, 'I think it's wonderful.' The grand duchess was no longer with us, and a faintly darker shade of pink stole across the nape of Mr Greenslade's neck. I also thought it was wonderful, but confined myself to saying, 'I'm sure you're right,' as in a sense I was. 'What happens next?' I said.

'Well, once he has the Sub-Committee's recommendation, Absolam will draft a resolution to be laid before the P.R. and G.P. and an Order to be issued by the Planning Committee on the basis of that resolution. Then that goes to the Ministry with an urgent request for provisional confirmation. It'll be all right. In any case, he'll be sure to let Mr Wainwright know it's on the way. He'll have seen the surveyor for that matter. And of course there's always the Forestry people. They'll get in first, as it happens, and they're more effective than we are, to tell the truth, in a case like this.'

'That's what Mr Absolam said. Anyhow, what do we do next?'

'Nothing more you can do, thanking you very much. Only watch it, of course. I don't think he can do much, but if there's any signs of suspicious activity, you'd better let me know at once. I'm in the book. Or Absolam. But it won't be Barretts' does the job, I'm pretty certain of that, and I imagine Wainwright can't do it himself. No, I think you'll find we've stopped him. Of course, he can lodge an objection to the Order, but I don't see what he can say that even the Ministry can see any sense in.'

We left Mr Greenslade at Lisburne. The drive home was completely silent. We were both in fact tired, but the tiredness was, on my side at least, a welcome refuge. The vultures were at my liver again, and I did not feel like talking. When we got in, Elizabeth said, 'You realise it's half past two, and we haven't had any lunch. Do you want anything?'

'I know. It was well after one when we left the Seele farm. That's why I suggested coming here first and dropping you. But little Greensleeves didn't want it, and I didn't want to upset him. I suppose he doesn't eat lunch.'

'Never mind. He's a pink precious treasure. I'll get some cheese for now, and we can have tea early.' We could have been cheerful fellow-campaigners, and I did not mind whether she was alive or dead. Or rather, I did. I minded very much indeed. For her part, she was full of barely-suppressed exhilaration, which she knew ran counter to my mood, but could not be bothered to conceal effectively. I did not think it was all to do with the trees, but I did not want to get close enough to it to examine it in detail. The food made me feel better, but I still could not think of anything I wanted to do. My whole life for weeks past had been focused on the next time I should see Carol. Now there was no edge to anything.

Elizabeth came back from the kitchen and said, 'Are you going into the wood today?' It was the first time she had asked me this and the first time I was able to reply truthfully. I said, 'I don't know. I hadn't particularly thought of it. Why?'

'Well – just to keep an eye on things. I badly want to know how things are developing.'

'I don't see what can happen today. By tomorrow Dennis may come under fire, but hardly today. But there's nothing to stop you going along the path if you want to. It's probably just when you're looking for the Rural District surveyor that you'll see *nycticorax*. Or do you think he's gone?'

'Either gone or very soon going. The important thing is that he can come to the wood again next year.'

'If Mr Absolam does his stuff, you'll be able to roll the red carpet right down the central pathway.'

She said, 'I'll be here, anyway.' She emphasised the pronoun. I remembered this later. At the time I felt merely that it was another slight discord, but my mind was not properly on what she was saying. She went marching off towards the wood, so full of triumph that it showed in her step. I walked down on to the beach and turned my face westwards. The wind was not blowing as strongly as it had the night before, and the sea was less noisy, but there might still be the same anodyne in it if I walked far enough. Only it was too early yet. I could not walk till bedtime.

I saw Carol first as a movement on the beach. She was wearing something grey which in that grey light blended indistinguishably with the colours of the stones. When I got her focused I saw that she was coming towards me. I do not know when she saw me. Almost certainly before I saw her. Her long sight was probably better than mine, and I was wearing darker clothes. For a long time we walked slowly towards each other along that endless, almost straight avenue between the tumbling grey sea and the green lip of the land. The meeting had a sort of symbolic inevitability, so that neither of us quickened our pace or did anything to anticipate the moment of meeting. Neither of us smiled. We watched each other gravely. We might have been protagonists in a Western, ready to draw on each other at the slightest sign.

We stopped a few feet apart and stood facing each other. She made no move to touch me, and I did not dare risk her displeasure by touching her first. She said, 'Hullo, Jake,' in the small, flat voice I had first heard from her. I stood there looking down at her. She said, 'Have you done anything about the wood?'

'Yes,' I said. 'Has anything happened at your end?'

'Nothing I can be sure of. Only I rather think he's having trouble with the contractors. They've put the job off a week, or something of that sort. He was very angry. But that's only what I gathered. I didn't hear anything specific.'

'It could well be. In any case, he's going to have the authorities after him. Both the Forestry Commission and the County Council. They'll probably show their hands tomorrow. I don't think he can go on with it. I fancy the contractors already know that.'

'Have you done that?'

'Elizabeth, in fact, mostly. She's very cock-a-hoop about it.'

She nodded. Then she said, 'What are you going to do?' She was no longer talking about the wood.

'I don't know. Only I can't leave things where they are. Something will give way. I suppose I could go away – altogether, I mean. Leave Elizabeth here, if she wanted to stay, but insist on going myself. I haven't really been able to think effectively at all. We'd better get the business of the wood settled first. But that's only a matter of days, really, I think. It's simply a matter of seeing what your husband does when he finds the authorities against him. If he accepts the position, the thing's over. Then there's nothing to keep me, here or anywhere else.'

She said, 'All right, Jake. Good-bye, for now.' Then she turned and walked off eastwards along the beach. She made a minute figure on the vast grey beach, and everything in the world dwindled with her.

It was nearly dark when I got home. Elizabeth was in the kitchen, boiling eggs for our tea because we had missed lunch. She was humming quietly to herself. She said she had seen nothing in the wood to interest her. Whether she had seen Carol walking back along the beach she did not say.

She was off to the wood again soon after breakfast next morning, and came back in a state of high excitement. She said, 'Everything's boiling up together. You should have been there. First there was a man from the Forestry Commission. The van was marked. He got out and walked round the wood for a bit, sniffing almost audibly. Then he got back into the van and ruffled papers for a bit, plans and things. Then he got out and went to the house. I was lurking in the trees across the road. There's quite a hide there. Did you know? You can see the whole front of the Wainwrights' house. I waited to see him come bouncing down the steps, like unwelcome callers in the comic strips, but nothing happened for quite a while. When he did come out, he opened the door for himself and came out quite quietly. I'll bet you anything Dennis was still in the study, biting the edge of his desk. The little man – well, he wasn't all that little really, but no match for Dennis – he came down and out of the gate. He was sweating slightly and running his finger round inside his collar. Honestly. I'm not making this up. And he had a small, rather satisfied smirk on his face, as if he had had the better of it, but was a bit shaken all the same. I didn't see Dennis at all. I waited a bit, but he never came out. Then as I was starting to come home, there was another man, actually in the wood. He had come along our track and left his car half-way along, and walked into the wood from that side. But he hadn't got very far. He was just peering about, looking at the trees. He didn't stay long. I don't know if he went to see Dennis too. It would have been an experience for both of them, wouldn't it, after the Forestry man?'

'If he was the Rural District surveyor,' I said, 'he wouldn't need to go and see Dennis, I don't think. All he's got to do is to confirm that the wood is as shown in the map and report on the state and value of the trees. I imagine they'll get this Preservation Order served by post.'

'Never mind. I'm sure our nice shaggy Absolam will tell us when it is going off. Perhaps I could watch the postman deliver it.'

'If I were you,' I said, 'I don't think I'd spend too much time in the wood – not in the far end of it, anyhow. I know you're proud of having started all this, but that may well have come out. Dennis's feelings towards you at the moment must be quite indescribable. All right,' I said, when she giggled at this, 'I know it gives you a kick, and I can't say I blame you. But in all seriousness, I'd watch out for Dennis, if I were you. I wouldn't trust that man with a stick in his hand more than I'd trust a sabre-toothed tiger with his mouth well open.'

She said, 'Do you really think he'd go for me?' She looked at me wide-eyed, but the apprehension was only half-serious, and there was a small unattractive streak of fascination in it.

'I don't know,' I said. 'But I don't regard him as suitable material for experiment. It's up to you, but I'd lay off the wood for a bit if I were you – unless, of course, *nycti* comes to hand suddenly.'

'But that's just it,' she said. 'He has. At least, I think he has. The absurd thing is that it was just as you said. In fact, it was more or less because of what you said. You know you said I'd be looking for the Rural District surveyor and find *nycti*. Well, when I saw him there, peering about at the trees, I remembered what you said and after he'd gone I had a good look in that part of the wood. And there is something there. I couldn't be absolutely certain, and I didn't want to disturb him. But I'm fairly certain there's something of about the right size roosting in one of the oaks. It's a good deal further up towards our track than I've ever looked before. I think he must shift his ground a bit. Anyway, I've marked the place, and I'm going to try it again this evening.'

'You seem to have had a good morning,' I said.

Her smile was almost a simper. 'Wonderful,' she said.

The ridiculous thing is that I do not know, now, whether the Tree Preservation Order was ever served on Dennis Wainwright. I suppose it must have been in due course, if not of law, at least of executive procedures. The cumbrous machinery we had short-circuited into unexpectedly rapid motion probably threw up its end-product. For the matter of that, the holm oaks are still there. I suppose Dennis must have been diverted once for all from his intention by the actions of the Forestry Commission. From then on events ran smoothly to catastrophe. I did not see Carol again during that time. The background of the whole nightmare was my apprehension for her, shut up in that horrible brick box with the frustrated and certainly enraged Dennis. But then I had been apprehensive for her before, and, apart from the look I sometimes caught on her face when her husband was mentioned, she never let up about the details of their relationship. If I had in fact seen her, even once, and got from her some inkling of what he had in mind, things might have ended differently. But as it happened I never did. And in any case she probably never knew.

It must have been two days after the Forestry Commission had delivered their warning that Elizabeth came running into the house somewhere between noon and lunch-time. I heard her calling 'Jake! Jake!' as she came up the path, and we met in the hall. She said, 'For God's sake come. There's a whole army of men disembarked at the far end of the wood with trucks and God knows what else. He can't be going to defy orders, can he? I can't bear it. Shall I phone Mr Absolam?'

'Wait a minute,' I said. 'Let me at least see what they're up to.' We went out along our track on the north side of the wood. I think we ran at times, I know I was hurried along by an almost frantic Elizabeth. There was, as she had said, a small army of men deployed round the farther end of the wood, but it did not take long to see what they were doing.

'It's all right,' I said. 'At least – I don't know what his game is, but these chaps aren't cutting anything. They're fencing.'

CHAPTER FOURTEEN

Elizabeth said, 'But he can't shut us out of the wood. Jake, he can't do that, can he?'

'He can't stop us using the path. He can keep us out of the rest of the wood, I suppose, if he wants to. If he's mad enough, he could fence round the wood and fence along both sides of the path. But it doesn't make sense. I don't know what he's up to. I tell you what, though. The test will be what he does at the ends of the path. If he puts up stiles or gates, it will show he doesn't intend to dispute the right-of-way. Anyhow, judging by the way they're working at the moment, these chaps are starting along the north side of the wood. At that rate the end of the path they come to first will be the one opposite us. If they fence that right across, I'll open fire at once. In the meantime, we must just sit back and watch it.'

'Can't I—?'

'No,' I said. 'No, Liz, you mustn't do anything at all. He's got a perfect right to fence round his wood if he wants to. And so long as the men don't go crashing about inside the wood, it's not going to upset *nycti* or anyone else. For goodness' sake, wait and see what they're up to. It will take them some time to get round, though I must say he's evidently told them to make a rushed job of it. When they're packed up this evening, we'll go along the track and see if we can see what they're doing. Until then do please keep clear.'

She had been riding high for days now, and did not like being crossed. She said, 'Oh well, if you think—' and melted away to the kitchen where she got ready a rather scrappy lunch. During the afternoon she took out her glasses towards the mere, but I knew they would be trained along the north side of the wood as much as across the water. At teatime she said, 'They're just putting posts in. They're being very slow.' Later, when it was almost dark, we walked out along our own private track on the north side of the wood, going as stealthily as if we were a mile inside a preserved park and heading for the pheasantries. They were, as Elizabeth had said, putting posts in. They were concrete posts, standing six feet clear of the ground and pierced for several lines of fencing wire. What they were in fact going to carry was not apparent. But it was a strong, professional and certainly expensive job. And it was going fast, for all Elizabeth's impatience. The posts were already nearly half-way along the northern edge.

The wind had died out completely. The grey dusk was silent and rather foreboding. On this side of the wood we could not hear the sea at all. I felt oddly like a besieged garrison, with the enemy creeping slowly round our defences. This was ridiculous when it was not us they were enclosing, but the sense of hostile forces moving towards us from the other end of the wood was very strong.

This went on for three days. We never saw Dennis Wainwright or had any contact with the men doing the fencing. We knew them all well by sight through the glasses, and Elizabeth gave them pet-names and took an interest in their personal relations, but we never had speech with them. This was mostly on my insistence, I think because I believed Dennis would expect us to question his workmen. But one thing was settled by late on the second day. He was not going to shut the path. At our end of the wood the fence was broken by a rather repulsive but perfectly reasonable concrete stile. There was no indication so far of any attempt to fence the path itself. The posts crept past the Holt House and rounded the corner of the wood above the beach. From now on we saw nothing of the men at all unless we went out on to the beach deliberately, which Elizabeth did at regular intervals. They worked from the road at the far end of the wood.

I forget how long it was before the posts were complete and they began to hang the fencing. It seemed quite a long time, and all the time the wind never blew above a whisper, and the men banged and shouted to each other in the grey silence. When the fencing started, we had the final answer. There was sheep-netting up to four feet, heavy two-way netting in six-inch squares, impermeable to anything much bigger than a cat. The two feet above it were covered by strands of barbed wire, set close and drawn hard. It was a formidable barrier. We still did not know what it was for.

They finished the job by lunch-time one day, and by mid-afternoon Elizabeth came back from the beach and reported that they had all packed up and gone home. She seemed almost mildly regretful, as if she missed the excitement. After tea we went out and for the first time climbed the concrete stile that gave access to the path. We tiptoed along the path into the middle of the wood. I remember thinking how seldom Elizabeth and I had been in the wood together. For all her passionate interest in *nycticorax*, I still found her presence there incongruous and for some reason uneasy.

That last calm of the autumn was still with us, and the wood was completely silent. All round us, invisible but making its presence felt, the wire frame shut us in. When we got to the other end of the path we found a stile similar to the one we had just climbed, but we did not climb it. Away to our left, and exactly where my observation post had been, there was a full-width gateway in the fencing, closed by a five-barred farm gate of steel tubes. Even the gate had wire mesh hung on it. I remember thinking the place was like a zoo, and for the first time a strong whiff of uneasiness crept into my mind about Dennis Wainwright's intentions in all these monstrous defences.

I said something to Elizabeth, in a whisper full of forced jocularity, about *nycticorax* being well protected from unauthorized intruders if his presence there became known. She took it quite seriously and agreed it might be a good thing. Fencing or no fencing, I believe she was still determined to make her recording and establish her observation. All I wondered about was Carol. But whatever Carol did, the wood was spoilt now. The ridiculous thing was that if it had been fenced from the start, I believe it would have made little or no difference to anything that had happened there. But by fencing it like this, now and in deliberate though still obscure defiance, Dennis had put his hand on it more indelibly than if he had patrolled the central path hourly in his John Bull breeches, swinging his heavy stick. Whatever happened to Carol and me, the wood was not ours any more. If Elizabeth and *nycticorax* still wanted it, they could have it.

We tiptoed out of the wood, Elizabeth still in a condition not much different from muffled hysteria, and myself full of an appalling disquiet I could feel no logical justification for. We left the wood behind us, hushed, completely enclosed and empty. I thought it was waiting for something, but I did not know what. We heard the telephone ringing as we came in at the gate and Elizabeth ran ahead to answer it.

She came out and said, 'Jake, it's for you. I think it's David Sangster.' David Sangster was the junior partner in the firm of solicitors I patronised. He was my sort of age and a friend of mine. He said, 'Jake? Jake, listen. We've had a letter from a chap called Wainwright. He's the man your uncle sold the wood to. Do you know the one I mean?'

I said I did. I asked how Dennis Wainwright had got on to them. 'Probably through Marples,' said David. Marples were my late uncle's solicitors. 'Anyway, he found us. Tell me, has there been any discussion of the possibility of your buying the wood from him?'

'I did make a very tentative suggestion. He wouldn't consider it at all.'

'Oh. Well, his letter here suggests that he may now be prepared to consider it. But it's a pretty odd letter. Look, Jake, I don't want to talk at length over the phone. I wondered if you could run up to town and have a word with me about it?'

'I could, yes, easily. Tomorrow, if you like.'

'Yes, I wish you would. I'm tied up for lunch, unfortunately. Will the early afternoon do?'

I said it would, and we left it at that. Elizabeth said, 'What did David want?'

'He wanted me to come up and see him some time. I gather there are odd points outstanding about Uncle Clarence's will he'd like to get sorted out. I said I'd go tomorrow. Do you want to go to London?'

She hesitated, pouting a little. 'Why the urgency?' she said. 'No. I don't want to be away a whole day just now. I might have liked it later.'

'We can go again,' I said.

'All right. You go tomorrow, then.' She was not really satisfied, and I could not blame her. It might be nothing, but I was not going to mention a letter from Dennis Wainwright to Elizabeth until I had seen what was in it. From David's tone, it did not sound disastrous, but he was apparently being a bit cagey over it, and my instinct was to be cagey myself.

Unless you wanted to do it by road all the way – Stella did regularly, but I found it unnecessarily tiring – the journey to London meant driving into Burtonbridge and getting an early train to town. There were trains back in the evening. It gave you a reasonable time in London, but it made a long day from Marlock. I was away by half past seven next day. It was a dark morning. There was still no wind at all, but I had a feeling that the calm was not going to last much longer. As I drove along its northern edge the wood looked pitch dark behind its new, white fence, but nothing looked at me through the wire. When I came to the gate on the road, I thought I saw Dennis Wainwright's head in the garden of his horrible house. It struck me as odd that I was going a hundred and twenty miles to look at a letter from the man across the road. It certainly never occurred to me to turn down the road and ask him what it was all about. I could not even be completely sure he was there. I turned left and drove to Burtonbridge.

David looked at me curiously over the tops of his glasses, but handed me the letter without comment. After introducing himself and saying he understood they were my solicitors, Dennis Wainwright had written:

'It is my wish that there should be no further personal contact of any sort between your client Mr Haddon and myself or any member of my family. As the existence of a right-of-way through my wood makes such contact very difficult to avoid, I am prepared to sell Mr Haddon the wood at the price I originally paid for it plus the cost of subsequent improvements' – this presumably meant the fencing – 'on the express condition that he undertakes to avoid all future personal contact with myself or any member of my family. In the alternative, I am prepared to pay for the extinction of his right-of-way at a figure to be agreed and on the same general conditions.'

It was written in a hand as big as the man himself, with fierce angles and heavy down-strokes. I looked up and met David's speculative eye. 'I don't know what you've been doing to him,' he said. 'That's your business. What does his family consist of?'

I looked at him blandly. 'So far as I know,' I said, 'only his wife.' David's eyebrows rose ever so slightly. Blandness was no good with David. He said, 'It's an unusual proposal, to say the least of it. I don't know how this no-contact condition would be enforceable. That depends on the way the contract was drawn, I suppose. If it made the whole sale voidable for a breach of condition, you'd have to be pretty careful. It looks to me as if you've got to be pretty careful anyhow. What do you want us to do about it, Jake?'

'I'll have to think,' I said. 'I'm grateful to you for getting me up to talk about it, David.'

'Yes,' he said. 'Yes, well, I thought I'd better, rather than simply pass it on to you through the post. All right, Jake. I'll acknowledge and say we are in touch with you and are awaiting your instructions. And you let me know what you decide. And as I say, be careful in the meantime. In any case, better not deal with him direct.'

'Not on your nelly,' I said. We exchanged chit-chat and he saw me off, still with a speculative look in his eye. I had an early dinner at my club and caught the last train for Burtonbridge. It was not a late train, but it would be late enough before I was home. By half-way I realised that the speed of the train was only partly responsible for the roaring forces outside the windows. We were running head-first into a gale. Whenever it had reached Marlock, our autumn truce with the weather was over. The beach would be chaos.

When I got out at Burtonbridge, it was dark as pitch and trying to blow the roof off the station. I pointed the car out of town for the Marlock direction, but that only made it worse. It must have been coming straight in off the sea. I was still five miles or more from home, and right in the middle of nowhere, when I found the tree across the road. It was on a straight stretch, and I saw it in plenty of time, but the road was blocked completely. No one else had found it yet. There were no lights. By now it was raining hard. Even with the car stopped, the rain came at the windscreen as if it had been shot from a gun. I opened the door, but shut it again at once. I had a raincoat of sorts, but my town clothes were no good against this. Getting the best observation I could through the rain-clogged glass, I started to back the car. It was on the second time back that I put her driving wheels in the ditch, and I knew at once that it was going to be no good. I tried, of course, and only dug her grave the deeper. It would have to be a tractor in the morning. I was not going to leave the lights on. There would not be anything out in these conditions, and the tree screened the car completely from one side and effectively from the other. I put my torch in my pocket and climbed out into the weather. I locked the car and walked back to the tree. Even for a pedestrian it was a pretty comprehensive obstacle, and I did not know what condition the main branches were in after the fall. I decided to go round through the fields. By the time I was back on the road again I had given up all thought of keeping any part of myself dry or any of my clothes clean. I put my head down and made what speed I could into the weather. Every now and then I needed a hand over my mouth if I was going to breathe. It was not dangerous or frightening. It was very tiring and ghastly uncomfortable. I remembered now that I had not given Elizabeth any time for my return.

She would not be worrying. There was nothing to think about, except the exhausting putting of one foot in front of the other.

It must in fact have been rather more than five miles to Marlock, and there was another quarter of a mile to go from there. I heard the roaring of the sea on the beach long before the dark mass of the wood showed up on my right. I looked down the road ahead, but the Wainwrights were showing no lights. I opened the gate and turned into the track along the side of the wood. The rain had stopped and here the trees gave me shelter from the worst of the wind. The wood roared in all its branches. After the tarmac, the track was full of potholes. My trousers and shoes were long past worrying about, but I did not want to break an ankle. I got my torch out and switched it on. All along in front of me, a few yards from the side of the track, the white posts and shining wire of Dennis Wainwright's fence stood out against the blackness of the wood. I was still not halfway along when my torch picked up the eyes inside the wire. There were quite a lot of them. They looked reddish and moved very fast.

I found myself standing dead still before I knew I had stopped. The eyes were still ahead of me, but the track stretched before and behind me into the darkness, and not far on my right the wind would be whipping up into foamless waves the unseen waters of the mere.

The more sensible part of my mind fastened on to the massive details of the fence. I have said it would be impermeable to anything much bigger than a cat. Whatever the eyes belonged to, they were very much bigger than cats. I pointed the torch at the wire about five yards ahead of me and started to go forward again. It was a moment or two later that something raced along the thin edges of the wood and shot through the torch beam. It was glistening wet and leggy, and ran zig-zag through the undergrowth. I had still not brought my mind to a sensible focus when I took the boar full in the light of the torch. He was enormous and reddish-brown, and as rangy as a mastiff. He carried huge tusks, and one of them, as he ran, flew a long streamer of something ripped out of the wood.

I was too tired now to think with any great coherence. After the big boar I saw several sows and later what looked like younger boars. The torch picked them up momentarily as they went charging through the dark tangle behind the shining wire. Whatever sound they made was lost in the roar of the wind. They were creatures of nightmare rather than ordinary beasts. I had had something to do with pigs at one time of my life, but never anything that looked and ran like this.

I went on down the track, flickering my torch sideways in the roaring darkness. I saw no more pigs. I still did not know what they were or where they came from. All I knew was that for his own obscene reasons Dennis Wainwright had turned them loose in the wood. He had fenced it and turned it into a private zoo for these creatures to run about in.

There was a light in the kitchen but nowhere else in the house. A note on the table said, 'Supper in the fridge.' I undressed completely and piled my sodden clothes in the sink. I ate something without much enthusiasm. Then I put the lights out and went to bed. I slept like the dead for exactly an hour and woke to find the wind screaming its head off round the house. It was only towards morning that I slept again and began to get the nightmares.

CHAPTER FIFTEEN

They came in a recurrent series, never exactly repeating themselves, but each one using some of the same elements and springing from the same desperate apprehension as its predecessor. I was impeded, always, by a wire fence higher and impossibly more complicated than Dennis Wainwright's. Each time I knew it was going to be there, but I could not remember who had put it there or when. Sometimes I was trying to get through it to something urgent beyond. Sometimes I was shut in by it, with unspecified dangers running about in the darkness behind me. Every time I woke up, or half woke up, in the middle of an inconclusive struggle with unnaturally elastic strands of wire.

I must have threshed about a lot and wrestled with the bedclothes, because it was cold that finally woke me. I had had nearly all the covers off me. It was a grey morning, still very early, and completely quiet. The wind had blown itself out, but left a chillier air than we had had yet. There was a moment of blankness, and then a cold wave of horror as tangible as cramp. I got up and ran across the landing into Elizabeth's room. She was not there and had clearly not been to bed at all. Her tape-recording gear, which she always kept together on a side table, was not there either. I ran back into my room and started to dress. It took a very long time, partly because I never seemed able to make up my mind what to put on next. I ran downstairs on stockinged feet, looking for my boots. As I started to put them on I said, 'Tamworths' aloud.

I suppose I had been trying to think what they were all the time, but last night my conscious mind had been too tired to make my subconscious give it up. Those creatures were Tamworths. They are a domesticated breed, but to the uninitiated eye more like wild pig than any domesticated creature has a right to be. Above all, they are rangy and fast-moving. I did not know if they were in fact any wilder than any other breed of pig. I had never had anything to do with them.

I looked round for a weapon and took up, of all things, an alpenstock. Why we had an alpenstock in the hall of the Holt House at Marlock I cannot think, except that it had always been in the hall wherever we lived ever since it came back from wherever somebody had first acquired it. It was in fact a very useful weapon, long, strong and iron-shod. I went out of the front door, down the flagged path and across to Dennis Wainwright's new concrete stile. I no longer ran. I found it increasingly difficult to face what I had to do, and whatever had happened had happened hours ago. Elizabeth had left my supper in the refrigerator and her note on the table not, as I had assumed, when she went to bed, but at dusk, when she went across to the wood with her tape-recorder. That was all of twelve hours ago. I climbed the stile, banging my iron-shod stick on the concrete with a clatter that went through the silent wood like a challenge. The debris of the storm was everywhere. I noticed, just before I lost it in the wood, the steady grinding roar of the swell breaking on the beach.

I went straight down the central path with no very clear idea in my mind. The dark earth was soft everywhere and in the hollows clinging mud. It was crossed and re-crossed with the marks of cloven feet. Some of them looked very big and deep. I did not hear any movement anywhere in the wood. I thought the herd was probably still asleep. It had not long been daylight.

I came within sight of the far stile, saw nothing on the path and turned back. About half-way along I struck off right-handed towards the northern side of the wood. Everything was wet, and before long my clothes were soaked almost to the waist. I made no more noise than I could help, but any sort of animal would have heard my movements a long way off. I was listening all the time for sounds behind me, despite the fact that it was on the northern edge of the wood that I had seen the herd rampaging last night.

I peered about me, not wanting to see anything different from the dark earth and tangled green. I was getting near the place where Elizabeth, according to her own account, had thought she had found *nycticorax* roosting. It was not far from the edge of the wood, and the ground was a little clearer. I saw something under a bush on my right, but did not go to see what it was. A moment later I almost stepped on the microphone with a trail of broken wire attached to it. It had been pushed down into the mud. After that I could no longer help looking at what I saw. Some of it was long strips, like the one I had seen the boar carrying on his tusks when he went charging through the torchlight. It was all scattered over quite a wide area. I tiptoed through to the edge of the wood, trying not to step on anything. Towards the edge, I hurried, but was brought up short by the wire, as I had been in my dream, although I had always known it was there.

I turned left-handed and went along for some way inside the fence before I turned back again towards the central path. At some point not far from the path I saw more blood and golden hairs, this time on the end of a single heavy stick. I picked it up and pushed the offending end deep into the mud. I was almost at the end of the path when I heard grunts and obscene scamperings away in the wood over my left shoulder. I still had my alpenstock, but had lost all apprehension of danger. A minute or two later the roar of the sea was so loud that I could not have heard movements except very close at hand.

It was only after I had climbed the stile that I started to run. I ran shouting half-way across the open space towards the Holt House before I realised there was no one there to shout to. Then I dropped to a walk, but I was still very short of breath. I tried to decide what to do, but was faced with the obscenely ridiculous difficulty of not knowing whom I ought to send for. When I was near the gate, Stella came round the north-east corner of the wall. She was carrying a suitcase and had plainly just got out of her car. She said, 'Hullo, Jake. Where's Liz?'

'She's in the wood,' I said.

She nodded and walked on up the path into the house. Then she put down her suitcase and turned round. 'Liz in the wood,' she said, 'at this hour?'

'Yes. It is early, isn't it? You must have come down overnight.'

She said, 'Jake, what's the matter? Is Liz really in the wood?'

'Liz is dead,' I said. 'Dead and more than dead. She's in the wood. I said so.'

Stella said, 'Sit down, for God's sake. I'll get you something.' She came back in a moment with a glass. 'Get this down,' she said, 'and stay where you are. Who do I phone?'

I looked at her blankly. I still did not know. 'I suppose the ambulance. And the police. Get the police, Stella. They'll know what to do, anyhow. Say there's been an accident, and Liz is dead in the wood.' She looked at me for a moment, standing over me with her head thrust slightly forward and her eyes fixed in their fierce, intense stare. Then she nodded and went to the telephone.

When she came back she said, 'Jake, what is all this? What do you mean, more than dead?'

'Pigs,' I said. 'Wainwright's put a herd of Tamworths in the wood. You've seen he's fenced it? They must have attacked Liz when she went in with her tape-recorder. I suppose she didn't know they were there. They've broken her up.' I looked up at her. I think my mouth and eyes were both wide open. 'Stella, they've broken her up completely. She's torn to ribbons. I had to walk—'

I put my head down between my knees and felt the blood come back. Stella said, 'Pigs. Oh my God, pigs.'

The police came half an hour later, apologizing for the delay. The road was blocked beyond Marlock, they said. They had had to go back and come in by the other road through Seele. Later, when they were busy in the wood, I phoned the Marlock garage and asked the man there to get the car pulled out of the ditch and driven to the Holt House. By the time he had her out, the tree had been cleared and the road was open.

I told the police, when they asked me, what my movements had been and what Elizabeth had been doing in the wood. I did not, of course, know exactly when she would have gone out there, but it would have been at dusk. They took it all down and went off to talk to Dennis Wainwright.

Stella moved into her room and took over the running of the house. She ran it much better than Elizabeth and made much less fuss about it. Whether or not it occurred to her that the arrangement was socially improper, we neither of us thought it worth mentioning.

The local Inspector came to see me next day. He was a big man – all country policemen are still fairly big men, though very few of them are any longer simpletons – with a pair of lifted eyebrows that gave him a permanently puzzled, deprecatory expression. He said the correct things briefly and got straight down to the heart of it. He said, 'I've been seeing Mr Wainwright, sir. I thought I'd better let you know the position – as we see it, that is. It's open to anyone to take a different view, of course. Now. The wood's Mr Wainwright's property and you've a private right-of-way across it. That's right, sir, isn't it? Just a private right-of-way, no public footpath?'

'Yes,' I said. 'The wood used to go with this property. When my uncle sold it to Mr Wainwright, he reserved a right of passage through the wood from this house to the road. I took over that right with the house, when my uncle left it to me.'

'That's right. Now. Mr Wainwright fenced the wood and put stiles at the end of the footpath. That was within his rights, of course. Then he put these pigs in. Seems an odd thing to have done. Do you know why he did it?'

His eyebrows came down suddenly. The effect was curiously topsy-turvy, and made him immediately formidable. I said, 'No, he didn't consult me. We saw he was fencing the wood, of course. We didn't know what for.'

He nodded. 'Well, there you are,' he said. 'Pigs are not animals you'd call normally dangerous. Not even this sort. Tamworths, they call them. I can't say I've ever seen them before.'

'Nor me,' I said.

'No. Well, as I said, for all they look a bit unusual, I can't find any evidence they're normally any wilder than other sorts. Of course, pigs can turn nasty on occasion, like anything else. But as I say, you wouldn't call them normally dangerous animals.' His eyebrows came down again and he looked hard at me. 'Now, sir,' he said. 'Mr Wainwright puts this herd in his wood. Mrs Haddon goes in, exercising her private right-of-way. Whether she went off the path on her own, or whether the pigs chased her off it, we can't say. But—'

'We can,' I said. 'You can take it that she went – where she was found – quite deliberately. There was an interesting species of bird roosting in the wood there, and she hoped to make a recording of its voice.'

'Ah, that was it. Well, anyway, the pigs turned on her and killed her. We can't say why. Now as far as the civil courts go, it's for you to take advice on any remedy you may have against Mr Wainwright. That's if you've a mind to. But so far as we're concerned, there doesn't seem to be any cause for action, unless Mr Wainwright did what he did deliberately. It's a matter of malice, do you see? He's within his rights putting his pigs in his own wood. But if he does it out of malice, with the intention of hurting you in your exercise of your right-of-way, that's different. If he set a trap, like, to catch whoever used the path. The question is, did he? Do you know of any reason why Mr Wainwright should entertain malice towards you? He doesn't admit any himself, as you might suppose.'

I looked at him and thought. It was still, after all, reasonable enough for me to be confused. I remembered telling Elizabeth to avoid Dennis Wainwright and his stick as she would a sabre-toothed tiger. I thought of Mr Absolam and Mr Greenslade. I saw in my mind's eye a stick, lying apart from the rest of the mess, with blood and hairs on it. I said, 'I don't know about malice. There had been some talk of his cutting the wood down, you know. We asked him not to. Then the authorities stepped in and stopped him. He would have been upset about that. It was after that he fenced the wood. But I don't see how you could prove malice. It's not as if he put a tiger on the path or killer dogs in the wood. We might have had no trouble with the pigs, I suppose.' I shook my head at him sadly. 'No, Inspector,' I said, 'I shouldn't like to examine Mr Wainwright's motives too closely, but I can't possibly prove malice. I don't like Mr Wainwright, and that's the truth. And after what's happened—' I shook my head again. 'But I can't prove malice, not deliberately malicious intention. Nor could you.'

He got up. It was not part of his job to look relieved, and he must have been born looking puzzled. He was almost certainly, in fact, a little of both, but he did not show it. He said, for the second time, all the proper things. He said, 'There'll have to be an inquest, of course. But we shan't do more than offer formal evidence. You'll understand that, sir?' I said I should, and he went off, leaving me to my freedom, my efficient sister-in-law and, to tell the truth, a considerable amount of delayed shock. The wind got up again and blew steadily from the west. So far as I knew, the pigs still ran about in the wood, but I did not go there. I had not given Dennis Wainwright's letter a thought. I wrote and told David about Elizabeth's death. He wrote back a very correct and sympathetic letter, but did not ask me for further instructions. I walked on the beach in the afternoons and there, two or three days later and a mile to the west of anything, I met Carol Wainwright walking to meet me.

CHAPTER SIXTEEN

I took hold of her hands. She did not avoid mine, but she put them decisively away from her. Her own hands were very cold. I said, 'Carol, Elizabeth's dead now. You know that.'

She stood there looking up at me, and when she spoke, it was in the voice I first remembered. Stella had called her a minute white woman with a voice to match. She said, 'Jake, what happened? I must know what happened.'

'You know as well as I do. She went into the wood with her recording stuff. I was away in London, but she must have gone into the wood in the evening, because that was when she hoped to get what she wanted. Your husband must have turned the pigs into the wood earlier that day, didn't he? I don't think they were there when I left in the morning. I suppose Elizabeth didn't know they were there. I got back very late. I'd ditched the car in the storm. I assumed Elizabeth was in bed. It was only in the morning I realised she hadn't been in her room all night. But in any case it was probably all over long before I got home.'

She shook her head very slowly from side to side. It was so like Dennis Wainwright's trick that it startled me, but that was silly. She had been married to him for long enough. 'But why?' she said. 'Why did they go for her like that? There was nothing to make them, unless— Pigs don't attack as a rule. You know that, don't you?'

'I don't know anything about Tamworths. With ordinary pigs – no, I agree. They don't attack unless there's something to set them off.'

'Blood,' said Carol. It was quite unexpectedly horrible, hearing her say it in that little flat voice. I suppose I had still got blood on the brain a bit. 'Blood,' she said again. 'If there's blood about, they go for it. Tamworths are no different. All pigs do it. She must have been injured first, or they wouldn't have done what they did.'

I said, 'You know that, do you? No one else has said so. It's true, of course. I've seen some terrible things with one of a herd accidentally injured. I didn't expect you to know. Does your husband?'

'Dennis? No, I don't think so. I don't think he knows anything about pigs except what he's just read up. Why should he? But you knew, didn't you, Jake?'

We stood there looking at each other for quite a while after that. We had been, to my immediate knowledge, the breath of life to each other after years of slow suffocation. Now we stood looking at each other through a barrier as translucent and impermeable as plate glass. I did not say, 'You can't think I killed her,' because it was obviously untrue. She could think so. Somehow or other I had to persuade her not to.

I said, 'But your husband had it in for her over those trees. He must have. He must have known it was mostly her doing that he was stopped. They'd have told him. I'd even warned her to be careful of him. I thought he was dangerous. Whether or not he knew the pigs might attack her doesn't matter. She could have been dead or dying before they touched her.'

'But Dennis didn't want Elizabeth out of the way. Why should he? You saw her as a barrier in your way – all right, Jake, in our way. But for Dennis she was a safeguard, for the same reason.'

'Only if he knew about us.'

'He did know about us. I told him.'

I stared at her. I felt something very like sheer physical nausea. I said, 'But—' Her face was quite expressionless. 'But you said he mustn't know. When did you tell him, Carol? I don't understand.'

'When I decided it was no use going on. It was the only way to stabilise things.'

A wave of the most appalling hopelessness rolled over me. I do not pretend to logic in the matter, but what I felt most clearly was a sense of betrayal. I said, 'Do you mean he accepted it?'

'I don't know what he did. He hasn't said or done anything.'

'He has, in fact. He wrote to me through my solicitor. Did you know?'

'No. How should I? When was this?'

'The day before Elizabeth died. No, two days before. Don't you see? He wrote to them and they rang up and asked me to go and see them.

That was why I went to London that day. I couldn't know I was going to run into trouble coming home – nobody could, for that matter – but as I say, the thing was done by then. Even if I'd got in at the expected time, Elizabeth would still have been dead by the time I got here. But it was his letter took me to London.'

'Did it have to take you to London?'

'It was a very odd letter. My solicitors would be very likely to want to discuss it with me, and in fact did.'

'He couldn't know you'd go up straight away like that.'

'He knew in fact I had gone. He was in the garden when I left. I saw him.'

'He couldn't know you were going to London.'

'At that time of the morning? Where else would I be going? Everyone gets the 7.40 from Burtonbridge.'

She gave me a look of such dreadful unhappiness that my whole heart melted towards her. She said, 'But I can't think he'd have done it. It's not only a matter of character. That might cut both ways, I admit. But I still don't see why he should.'

'Where was he that evening?'

'All right, I don't know. Not in the house, but I don't know where.'

I nodded. 'Leave it for the moment,' I said. 'About me. You talked about character. Do you think it is in my character to have done it?'

She had drawn back away from me again. She spoke in her small, dispassionate voice, looking at me from what seemed a great distance. 'I think you could, yes. Not by premeditation, probably. More in a moment of extreme frustration, even irritation. You wanted her dead, Jake. All right, so did I. Nothing else would do. But it's no good if you killed her.'

I shook my head despairingly. 'I didn't,' I said. 'Of course I wanted her dead. When you laid down the terms you did, I knew nothing else would do. Now that she is dead, and by no act of mine, I want you to leave your husband and marry me as soon as you decently can. But if you won't until you are convinced I didn't kill her, I shall have to try and find out what really happened. Will you at least suspend judgment and give me a chance to do that?'

She said, 'If Dennis killed Elizabeth, I'll do whatever you like. But I must know. Now let me go. You mustn't come back along the beach with me, or even after me. You must turn inland and go home by the mere.' She left me as abruptly as she always had, even when everything had been perfect between us. I did as she wanted. I walked up the beach and over the coarse grass of the narrow strip that was neither beach nor land. When I came to the first of the stone walls that bounded the fields, I turned right until I came to a gate. Then I crossed the field and went eastward again, looking for another gate. By the time I had made my distance eastwards, I had the cold flat water of the mere between me and the Holt House. Then I turned south and made for the road.

It was a dark, appallingly dreary afternoon. As I came down towards the gate, I saw Stella standing at the top of the path that led down to the beach. She was quite motionless, silhouetted against the grey sky that ran down to a grey invisible sea. For some reason or other the words *Dido, with a willow in her hands, upon the wild sea banks* came into my head. The setting could hardly have been less suitable. As I watched her she turned and came back up the path.

She said, 'Oh hullo, there you are. I somehow didn't think you'd gone inland.'

'I'm a bit off the sea-side,' I said.

'Well, yes.' We turned in at the gate together. 'But there's no need to stay here, is there? You won't, will you, not after this?'

'I don't know. I haven't really thought about it.' 'But Jake—'

I had gone into the hall first and switched on the lights. It was not dark yet, but the house needed light. There was a quality, almost of desperation, in her voice that brought me round to face her. She stood a step lower than I did, looking up at me with the light direct on her face. The eyes were dark with tiredness and the cheekbones sharply modelled.

'It was Elizabeth wanted to stay here, not you,' she said. I noticed that ever since Elizabeth's death Stella had always spoken of her by her full name, never the shortened form. It had a curiously depersonalizing effect. Elizabeth was already less an active element in our lives than a historical figure, sterilized by time.

'No, not entirely,' I said. 'I told you I was not unhappy here, not in the place as such, I mean. I may move now, of course. But I'm not desperate to get away.'

'This thing with the wood is settled, isn't it? There's nothing else to keep you here, is there?'

There came clearly into my mind the picture of a small figure, made tiny by the huge stretch before and behind it, walking steadily eastwards along the beach in the grey afternoon and another figure, tall and quite motionless, up there on the wild sea banks, watching it go by. 'I somehow didn't think you'd gone inland,' Stella had said when she turned from her waiting and came up the path. I had wondered why at the time. I said, 'I don't feel like making any decision at the moment, that's the truth.'

'But you haven't got to make a decision. There's no hurry about that. All you want to do is get away from this place, even temporarily. Go to London for a bit. You could stay at your club, couldn't you?' She came into the hall and went past me, head back, looking straight in front of her. She had never had Elizabeth's rather calculated grace of movement. She moved either hesitantly or as if she was forcing her way through unseen obstructions. Now she shouldered her way through the empty air between me and the kitchen door as if she was an ice-breaker in heavy pack-ice. 'I'll think about it,' I said. I said it to her back, and she nodded briefly and disappeared into the kitchen.

Tea was a silent meal, but then so, without embarrassment, were most of my meals with Stella. After tea a growing restlessness drove me out into the wood. It was the first time since Elizabeth's death. The light was going. I took a torch and the alpenstock. I took the alpenstock with elaborate casualness, but Stella was nowhere about and nobody saw me go. I climbed the stile, taking care, this time, not to drum on it with my staff. The wind blew in off the sea, and I moved, as always, under a roof of faint continuous sound, but all round me the wood was silent. I felt very strongly that it was empty, and that Dennis Wainwright had herded his Tamworths into a stock lorry and sent them back to wherever they had come from. But I did not know, and my conscious mind argued caution. I turned towards the north side of the wood, going as quietly as possible.

It was already not easy to be certain of the place, even when I came to it. The men who had gone out there had done their work with a sort of gloomy and scandalised thoroughness. We had had two nights, at least, of rain, and, wherever they were now, the pigs had gone over the ground at intervals, trampling everything into neutrality. There was blood now in the composition of the soil, but were there ten yards of land anywhere in southern England where the blood had not, at one time or another, called from the ground for vengeance? I do not know what I expected to find. I thought that, knowing as I did what must have happened, I might be able to find some evidence of it. In particular, I wanted to recover the heavy stick I had myself pushed into the ground. I went about the place silently, head down, looking but not touching anything. It occurred to me that I should present to an observer an almost classic picture of the guilty creature returning to the scene of his crime. But there was no observer and there had been, officially at any rate, no crime. I went off, as nearly as I could, on the line I had followed that dank early morning after the storm, starting along the fence on the north side of the wood and then turning inwards towards the central path. I did this several times, advancing my turning point slightly each time, but keeping the same line of movement south-westwards. I knew I had driven the end of the stick fairly solidly into the earth. I thought that was probably the top of the stick, as it had grown on the tree. If I could only get within sight of it, it ought to have the conspicuousness of an unnatural object in the natural tangle of the wood. No dead branch falling from its tree would drive itself into the earth as far as that or at that particular angle: and no stick grows upside down.

The odd thing is that when I did come to it, I remembered the place first and found the stick because I particularly looked for it. As I had thought, there was no mistaking the artificiality of the angle once you had seen it. The stick itself was a natural waste product of the wood, but an oak stick, even a stick from a holm oak, is massive compared with the quicker growing hardwoods. It looked a handy enough weapon to pick up casually. It was not a cut cudgel. I put out my hand to pull it out of the soft earth, and almost at once heard movements from the direction of the central path, not ten yards away. The feeling I had had before of suppositious guilt came over me strongly. I took my hand back, straightened myself and turned cautiously in the direction of the sounds. I could see nothing, but there was someone there. The sounds were clearly human sounds. It is difficult to say why this was obvious, but there was never any doubt about it. I did in fact take a tighter hold on the alpenstock and get it balanced ready for action. But it was Dennis Wainwright I was afraid of, not the big boar.

The sounds had stopped again, and I decided to make a move myself. So long as I had not been seen on the prowl, there was no great harm in my being where I was, and I badly wanted to know who else it was in the wood with me. I moved cautiously towards the path. I found that so long as I went carefully enough, the noise of the wind in the tops of the trees provided a reasonable cover for any sound I made. I hoped that whoever it was on the path had not heard my rather hesitant movements a dozen yards to the north of him. He could not have been making much attempt to conceal his own.

When I came out on to the path, I could see no one in either direction, but I thought whoever it was had moved westwards, in the direction of the Holt House. Obviously to move after him down the pathway invited an ambush, but it also made it possible, in that breathing, rustling wood, to move almost completely inaudibly. I did not believe, in fact, that he knew I was there. There was no reason why he should turn aside and wait for me, and the jinks in the path ought to make it possible at some point to get a sight of him without being seen. Using the alpenstock as a walking stick and moving as quietly as seemed reasonably possible, I made off westwards along the path.

There was a disconcerting moment when I saw the stile, with the last of the daylight behind it, ahead of me, but no figure between me and it. He must have turned off the path one way or the other, and for all I knew I might have walked straight past him. I stopped and spun round, half expecting to find him on my tail, but there was nothing on the path behind me. I was getting tired of playing hide-and-seek. I decided to walk straight down the remainder of the path, where I had at least every legal right to be, get over the stile and go home. It was getting dark in the wood now, and even if I saw the enemy, I might not be able to recognise him. It was time to cut my losses and break off the engagement.

I walked to the stile, going steadily but fairly quietly, half turned to climb it and saw the figure of a man standing in the western edge of the wood a few yards to my left. He stood with one hand on a tree trunk and the other in his pocket, leaning slightly forward and staring intently at the front of the Holt House. The last of the daylight just touched his face. There was no mistaking the elegant figure and splendid, jutting profile. It was Mr Grainger of Seele.

CHAPTER SEVENTEEN

He would in any case have seen me when I got over the stile and walked across to the house. Whether I should, if I could, have pretended not to see him I do not know. I was still in two minds when the alpenstock clattered sharply against the stile and he spun round as if he had been shot at from behind. He had only seen me once, of course, in the driving seat of the car with Mr Greenslade beside me, but the number of people he was likely to meet in the wood at that hour was strictly limited. He knew me at once, and made a very creditable effort to get on some sort of reasonable terms with me before either of us started talking. I thought I was prepared to like Mr Grainger, even across the barrier of his physical graces.

I said, 'Mr Grainger, isn't it?' I put my ridiculous staff against the stile behind me. I saw that he was empty handed, and the thing embarrassed me.

'Yes,' he said, 'Mr Haddon, of course.' He took his hand away from the tree and came a few steps towards me. Then he stopped. 'It's no good,' he said. 'I can't think of any conceivable reason why I should be here that you'd be likely to believe. In any case – well, there it is. I was looking for your sister-in-law, Miss Lancaster.' He stopped and looked at me in the dusk. Then he said, 'It seems an odd place to exchange formalities, but may I say how sorry I was to hear of your wife's death?'

'Thank you,' I said. 'I confess myself interested to know why you should think that is a formality.'

He smiled. He had, as had been apparent from the first moment I saw him, a good deal of cheerful insolence in him. It would not endear him to many of the people he dealt with locally, particularly the husbands and fathers whose peace of mind his mere appearance must chronically threaten. I did not see it could do me any harm. He said, 'Put it down mostly to unfortunate phrasing. Apart from that – I have in fact only one source of information about you and your household.'

'Stella?' I said.

'Stella, of course.'

'And Stella's view was that any commiseration with me on the score of my wife's death was in the nature of a formality?'

'I don't think she ever said so in so many words. That was certainly the impression she conveyed. I don't expect you need to be told that there wasn't much love lost between them.'

'I don't, no. But Stella's opinion of her sister is not necessarily the same as my own.'

'Not necessarily, of course. Only I don't think in fact Stella believed them to be very different. That may have been wishful thinking on her part.'

He looked at me, one eyebrow raised and the ghost of a smile on his strong, slightly contemptuous mouth. I could not think why he wasted his time farming and being a County Councillor. Perhaps, as Mr Greenslade had said, he had political ambitions. Perhaps he did not photograph well. 'However,' I said, 'I think you were saying you had come to see Stella when we allowed ourselves to be diverted by formalities. I did not know, until you said so to my wife the other day, that you knew her. I don't think she has ever spoken of you.'

'No?' he said. 'No, perhaps not. We haven't known each other very long in fact.'

'Only since we came to the Holt House, I imagine? Or had you known her before?'

'No, no. Only since you came here. We met by chance, in fact, on one of her journeys down here, and I've seen her several times since.'

'And you want to see her again now?'

He put his hands in his jacket pockets and spread his feet a little apart. We stood facing each other. He was one of the few people I have known on whom slightly larger-than-life gestures sat naturally and who habitually used them with assurance and success. For my part I stuck my hands in my trouser pockets and waited. It was not me that had to do the explaining. He said, 'I had hoped I might see her, yes.'

'You know your own business best, Mr Grainger,' I said, 'but my sister-in-law's unmarried, an orphan, well over twenty-one and a successful professional woman. If you want to see her, there is no reason I know of why you shouldn't come to the door and ask for her. It is no business of mine to ask you your intentions. Not, at any rate, on the score of morals or ordinary prudence. If there's anything criminal involved, or if my sister-in-law is likely to get hurt, I might have something to say, because I happen to be very fond of her and concerned for her. Otherwise it's nothing to do with me. And as there's no one else about, I don't see why you should lurk on the edge of the trees like a love-sick wood nymph. Apart from anything else, I don't think you're well suited to the role.'

He laughed very pleasantly. 'I'm glad to hear you say you're fond of Stella and don't want her hurt. May I ask you, that being so, not to tell her you've seen me and spoken to me? I'm sorry if this seems odd, but you'll have to take my word for it that it will be far better – for Stella, I mean – if you don't. Nothing criminal involved, I assure you. As you say, she's quite capable of looking after herself – in most respects, anyhow. But she will be much happier if she doesn't know that I was here and that we met like this. Can I count on you?'

I said, 'Mr Grainger, you exasperate me much less than might have been expected. All right. I won't say a word to Stella. I suppose you know what you're up to. Now I'll get on, or she may be wondering where I am.' I recovered the alpenstock, rather unwillingly, from behind me and climbed over the stile with determined dignity. On the other side I stopped and said, 'I suppose there's nothing I can do? I mean – don't know what it is you want, but can I in any way help you to it?'

He was already a little way down the path, and there he too stopped and turned. He thought about it. This was clearly genuine. He really was considering whether or not he could make use of me. Finally he came down against it. 'No,' he said, 'I'm afraid not. But thank you very much, all the same. You'll be leaving here soon, I imagine? If not, I hope we meet some time.'

He strode off along the path into the darkness. He strode as he did everything else, a little too well to be true, but it was a magnificent exit. My own entrance to the Holt House, trailing the alpenstock, was less impressive. It was observed by Stella, who stood in the lit hall with the front door open. She said, 'Where have you been, Jake? Not the wood?'

'Yes,' I said. 'I thought it was time I had a look at it.'

'You're not worried about anything, are you?'

'About what, for instance?'

'Elizabeth's death.'

'That's rather a comprehensive question, isn't it?' I smiled at her but she was in deadly earnest. 'I regret the manner of her dying very much.'

'But not her death, Jake surely? You're not going to tell me you'd have her back if you could? She hasn't meant anything to you these three years at least. Except a pain in the neck.'

'All right, Stella. She hasn't. And no, I wouldn't. At least do me the justice to admit I've never said so. I never supposed for a moment that you were under any illusions about the marriage, but at least I've never burdened you with intolerable confidences.'

She said, 'I don't think the confidences would have added much to the general intolerability. I suppose you'd say you were being loyal. All it looked like to me was a simple refusal to face facts.'

'It wasn't the facts I refused to face. It was the consequences that would have followed from facing them. If a situation is genuinely intolerable, action can't be avoided, obviously. So it's easier not to admit that it is, even if it involves standing on your head blindfold. Most men – well, quite a lot of men, anyway – spend a remarkable amount of their lives standing on their heads blindfold. The very young won't do it, and are therefore branded by their elders as intolerant. In fact they are only more honest. But I'm not as young as all that, and I couldn't help myself.'

I turned from the hall into the sitting-room on the right. Stella followed me in there and, when I sat down, sat down opposite me. She said, 'If Elizabeth's death doesn't worry you, why go into the wood?'

I had never had much resistance to Stella's questioning, and I could not, like Elizabeth, take refuge in a lost temper. I said, 'I'm not worried by Elizabeth's death. I'm worried about it – about how it happened.'

'The pigs? That was ghastly, Jake, I know. But it was pure accident. Or do you think that man really put them in the wood deliberately?'

'Of course he put them in deliberately. But not to kill Elizabeth or anyone else. Just to scare us off. He wanted to spoil the wood for us.

Otherwise why choose that rather alarming breed? No, I don't think the pigs were intentionally murderous in themselves. But I think they helped no end.'

'Helped? I don't know what you mean, Jake. They killed her, didn't they?'

I could feel the intensity of the eyes I avoided meeting. 'I don't know,' I said. 'I'm not sure.' She moved suddenly, and when I looked up, she was half-way to the door.

'I must get supper,' she said. 'Do you mean you think Dennis Wainwright attacked her and the pigs merely broke her up? I think that's crazy. And in any case—' She spun round where she stood by the open door, and we looked hard at each other. 'In any case,' she said, 'why worry? It's done, isn't it? And you wouldn't have it undone, you admit that. Why dig about, for God's sake? I can't see any sense in it. I don't see it matters to anybody what Dennis Wainwright did. The great thing is Elizabeth's dead. Why can't we get away from here and forget the whole business?'

She did not slam either door, but she went from the sitting-room to the kitchen with an unnecessary violence of movement, bumping the corner of the hall table as she went. Elizabeth might have slammed the door, but she would have gone with a whisk of skirts and would not have hit the table. I was more than ever glad of Elizabeth's death, but beginning to be worried about Stella. I could not shut my mind to Stella, as I had shut it to her sister. If she was unhappy, I suffered with her. If she behaved badly, she hurt me, directly and sometimes fiercely. Her incisive mind and direct speech had for so long been my safety valve against mounting frustration and boredom, that I had failed to see how much the mere presence of Elizabeth was, in its turn, an insulation against Stella's penetrative and disturbing activity. Carol occupied almost the whole of my mind. With Elizabeth safely relegated to its outer edges, it was possible to maintain the curious balance in our relations which I had several times noticed with a certain amount of sardonic amusement. Stella was quite a different matter. I had surprised myself, when I had hardly done more than see Carol, by finding that I was not anxious to have Stella around. Now, with Elizabeth dead and Stella able to achieve an uninterrupted command of my attention, the thing threatened to be very uncomfortable indeed. It struck me as odd that a wife should offer less of a mental obstacle to a love affair than her uncommitted sister. Nevertheless, it was undoubtedly true, and I did not like it.

Over supper Stella said, 'I was wondering. Did anyone know you were going to be away that evening?'

'Only Elizabeth. And she didn't know when I should be back, because I forgot to tell her which train I was coming on. I know, because when I ditched the car and had to walk, I remember being glad I hadn't given her any particular time to expect me. But Dennis Wainwright saw me go off in the morning and had good reason to think I was going to London. It wouldn't have been difficult for him to go from there to the fact that I shouldn't be back until fairly late. I mean – if Elizabeth was killed when I imagine she was, I could hardly have been back from London by then, whatever train I came by. Not unless I had pretty well done my business on the platform at Waterloo. My ditching the car was irrelevant really, except that it meant I didn't find her until next morning. If I had got in less late and less tired, I might not have assumed so readily that she had gone to bed. But the thing was done by then. Or so I assume. I suppose it's possible that she might have been injured during the evening and not attacked by the pigs until later that night. But I don't think so. They were rampaging in that part of the wood when I got back.'

'Where did you ditch the car?'

'Well on the far side of Marlock. Five miles at least, I should think. There was a tree down blocking the road. I tried to back and turn but got in the ditch and couldn't shift her.'

I looked at her, wondering. She got up and started to shift the things. I pushed my chair back and said, 'It didn't hold you up, anyhow.'

'No. It was clear by the time I came through. They must have cleared it.'

'I wondered whether you had come in by the other road, through Seele.'

'Seele? No. Why should I come by Seele?'

'No reason at all,' I said. 'The Marlock road's more direct. I only thought you might have.'

'No,' she said, 'no. You go on through. I'll get coffee.'

I was up early next morning and caught Mike Grainger before he had breakfasted. He was supervising the milking of a beautiful Guernsey herd. He moved among their sleek perfection with a sort of appraising good-fellowship. He had long ago adjudged himself best beast in the show, and wore his blue rosette with the ease of established custom. He said, 'Hullo, Mr Haddon, you're up early.'

I was, in fact, up earlier than usual, but I resented the implication that a townsman like myself might have been expected to be still in bed. I was wide enough awake, at least, to apprehend the wariness under the practised charm. He walked out with me to my car, tiptoeing over the mud of the lane as I had seen surgeons tiptoe over the spotless but asterile corridors outside the operating theatre. 'What can I do for you?' he said.

I said, 'You know the night of my wife's death?'

He stood quite still. 'I can't remember, without looking it up, what the date was,' he said. 'But I know the night you're talking about, of course. It was the night we had the storm.'

I nodded. 'Did you see my sister-in-law that night?'

He said, 'Oh dear, oh dear.' The playfulness was not wholly assumed. He was mildly rueful at my question, but not seriously disturbed. 'Why do you ask, Mr Haddon?'

'You mean what business is it of mine?'

'No. Oh no.' He was suddenly in earnest. Humanity flowed startlingly out of him, and I knew, as I had known the evening before, how easy it would be to like him. 'No,' he said again, 'I didn't mean that, really. I think you are concerned. At least I think you should be. But I really did wonder what had made you ask about Stella's movements that night. I imagine it was something she said.'

I said, 'She arrived at the Holt House fairly early next morning. I assumed she had travelled from London overnight. I'm not sure, but I think she allowed me to assume this. I'm now inclined to believe that she came in fact from Seele.'

'All right. She did. She came down here the evening before. She dined with me and spent the night here. It was previously arranged. It wasn't the first time.'

I nodded. 'Did my wife know about this?' I asked.

'About this particular fixture? I don't know. She knew about us, yes. Stella told me. I don't know how she found out. But it needn't have been particularly difficult, if she was sufficiently interested. Stella and I are both, as you said yesterday, free agents. There was nothing particularly clandestine about it. Only—'

For the second time in my experience of him Mike Grainger was genuinely at a loss. He became immediately and enormously more likeable. 'Yes?' I said.

'Only she didn't want you to know, Mr Haddon. That above everything. It was very important to her that you shouldn't.'

'She told you that?'

'Oh yes. There was no reason why she shouldn't, after all. As you know, I did my best, not very successfully, to see that you didn't. Hence the love-sick wood nymph act. I thought that was a little unkind of you, I must say. I was trying to do right by everyone. It never pays, of course. I shouldn't have attempted it if it hadn't been something pretty important.'

'It was important?' I said.

He looked at me. His face was friendly but quite blank. 'Oh yes,' he said, 'it was very important indeed.'

CHAPTER EIGHTEEN

I beat Stella to it by a split second when I got in. 'I was up early,' I said. 'I couldn't sleep much.' This was true enough. I had seldom passed a night more miserably.

She said, 'Jake, this is nonsense. You've never looked anything but awful since you came to this place. For God's sake make the break now. You could get a flat or something if you want to be on your own. I ought to be in London now anyhow, and I could do whatever you needed until you decide what to do permanently. Can't you make up your mind to it?'

'Give me twenty-four hours,' I said. 'God knows I don't want to be a burden to you.'

'All right. But I'll hold you to it. This time tomorrow.'

I finished completely, but almost without noticing it, the admirable breakfast she provided. I noticed that whatever else I suffered I seldom really lost my appetite. I had lost weight because my agitation and restlessness burnt up fuel at a surprising rate. But I seldom failed, during the whole time I was at the Holt House, to eat fairly regular and solid meals, whatever I lacked in sleep or mental quiet. Perhaps it was the sea air, but I cannot honestly recommend it.

I wanted to go to the Wainwrights' end of the wood, but I did not want Stella to know where I was going. It was all a rather dreary business. I minded deceiving Stella much more than I had ever minded deceiving Elizabeth. Also, she was much harder to deceive, I suppose because she, too, felt more strongly than Elizabeth ever had. I pottered out of the gate northwards and went down to the mere.

The mere had always been Elizabeth's preserve, ever since the first evening we had got here and she had picked her room to overlook it. I did not like it at all. In this grey autumn weather it was almost actively repellent, flat but always wind-ruffled, fresh water more or less, but scurfed round the edge with the salt that came in with the wind and seeped through under the beach. I picked my way eastwards along its southern side, out of sight of the house under the steep bank. At its eastern end it reached as far as the eastern end of the wood, but I did not go that far. About half-way along I clambered up the bank until I could see both ways along the track. There was no one about. The Holt House had retired behind the corner of the wood. I climbed out on to the track, crossed it and set about, for the first time, climbing Dennis Wainwright's fence.

It was not at all like my dream. So far from being elastic and clinging, it was as rigid as a climbing frame. The only difficulty was the barbs on the top strands, and I was in no particular hurry, once I was reasonably out of sight of either end of the track. I climbed with elaborate care up one side, teetered for a moment while I got my legs over the top, and then climbed down the other. It was not even, from a human viewpoint, a very effective barrier. If ever *nycticorax*'s haunt was discovered, this would not keep the enthusiasts or predators out. The only things it had been put up to contain had run for perhaps three days inside it, and done their work, and been carted away again. It was an odd business, and a shocking waste of money.

I thought of going back for the stick, which I knew I could find again, but it was the eastern end of the wood that drew me. There was extraordinary little sign of the pigs. I edged up towards the side of the gate, where my hide had been, and saw Carol standing in the upstairs window. She was there only for a second. Then she turned and went back into the room. I did not think she could possibly have seen me. I was desperate to speak to her, but did not know what I could safely do. Dennis Wainwright might be in Burtonbridge or London, or he might be round the next corner of the red-brick wall. He might, most probably, be in his dark study at the back of the house, sitting behind his empty desk and thinking about I did not know what.

I climbed over the gate and walked slowly down the tarmac. I had a right to be there and did not think he would be likely to shoot me down in daylight on the public highway. I had got past reasoning. I merely went from point to point, like a desperate man wading into a river he has got to cross if he can, content to try again so long as the last step has not carried him away.

I walked to the small front gate, put a hand to open it and then stopped dead. Dennis Wainwright was in the front garden. He was on his hands and knees, working on a flower bed under the front window. Most of what I saw was his behind, massive and uncompromising in almost black trousers. The seat of the trousers was polished with much sitting. It was evidently one of his extraordinary dark suits, relegated to gardening after he had rubbed the nap off it sitting at his desk. Occasionally he swung a little sideways, and I had a glimpse of the great head, under its heavy grey thatch, bent down over the earth of the tiny suburban bed. He muttered to himself as he worked, but I could not hear what he said.

Something happened, and he sat back suddenly on his heels. He had some green thing in his hands. I think he must have broken something by mistake. He had a green half in each big grey hand and shook his head over it, muttering. He even tried, as a child might have done, to fit them together again, but desperately, as if he knew it was no use. For a moment he knelt there, quite disconsolate. He was a ridiculous figure. Then he threw one half of whatever it was away with a savage and unnecessary violence and bent to put the other back into the bed. He sighed as he stooped over it, a sigh of such intensity that it travelled visibly backwards along his bowed body and swayed the high lights on the polished seat of his trousers.

I left the gate and stepped back into the road. I had rubber soles but had not come with any conscious effort at quietness. Now I backed away as from a land-mine, straight back across the width of the road until I was well hidden under his front hedge. Then I turned, even then reluctantly, and tiptoed to the stile at the end of the footpath. I remember noticing that it was of a slightly different pattern from the stile at our end. There was no significance in the difference. It was merely as if the contractor had not happened to have two exactly similar stiles in stock. It offended my sense of symmetry, but I did not linger over it.

It was only when I was in the wood that I noticed that the wind was getting up again. It is possible that the wind had only then, in fact, arrived, or the eastern end of the wood may have been largely sheltered by the great bulk of the trees stretching away behind it. But now the wind was everywhere. As usual, it did not make much noise under the trees, but it made a continuous background of restless sound in the top branches. It covered the noise of anything moving in the wood, and I was glad the pigs were no longer there. The noise I did hear was quite close to the left-hand side of the path before I heard it. I stopped, and a moment later Carol came out from among the trees ahead and turned along the path to meet me. She was breathless as if she had been running. So in fact she must have been. She must have gone down on to the beach, or even crossed the road lower down, while I was standing at the gate and come in to head me off. I did not know how long I had stayed at the gate, but it could not have been long between the time I saw her in the window and the time I climbed back over the stile into the wood.

She said, 'Jake. Jake, I mustn't stay. He comes into the wood quite often now, and he will if he finds I'm gone. I saw you standing at the gate. I was afraid. I didn't know what he'd do if he saw you. I tried to signal to you, but you were watching him. I couldn't make a sound. It was like a nightmare. I thought I'd head you off in case you went through the wood. But I didn't really think you'd come this way.'

She gave me her hands and we stood like that, looking at each other. She got her breath slowly, and when she spoke again, it was much more like her usual voice. She said, 'Do you think you know what happened? Your wife, I mean.'

'Not yet. Not to be certain. But Carol, for God's sake—'

She was not listening to me. Her eyes were over my shoulder, staring at their end of the wood. She whispered, 'I don't know – I thought – Jake, I must go. Can you meet me on the beach this evening? Just below the trees, about half-way along. I can get out then for a bit. About half past five. Then it will be dark before I'm home. Please, Jake.' She took her hands out of mine and ran off through the wood. She ran southward, towards the beach. She never made much noise at any time, but now the sound of her going was swallowed almost at once by the noise of the wind in the tops of the trees. The whole wood seemed full of movement. I stood still for quite a long time, waiting for a sound which I did not want to hear, and which never came. But there were sounds everywhere. It was still not mid-morning, but the wood was surprisingly dark. What with the darkness and the whispering, it might have been full of people, but there was no one to be seen. I walked off steadily along the central path, trying not to run. I wished I had my ridiculous alpenstock, but it would have been no use against what I felt was in the wood.

I was almost at the end of the path when I remembered that when I had left the Holt House, I had gone northwards, by the mere. I did not want to be seen coming back from the near end of the wood. I went cautiously to the end of the path and looked out, but could see no one. Then I turned northwards, just inside the edge of the trees, and picked my way back to the track. It meant climbing the fence again, but I knew now that this was no great obstacle. I crossed the track a little way along the top of the wood, just out of sight of the house, and made my way back under the bank of the mere.

When I got to the gate I found Stella standing just inside it. She was looking across to the wood and hardly seemed to notice me when I came down the road. The noise of the sea was everywhere now, and she may not have heard me.

I said, 'It's blowing up again.' She nodded but said nothing. She was still staring at the wood. I went past her and into the house, and presently she followed me in. The house was as dark as the wood had been. The line *To the dark house and the detested wife* kept running in my head. Only I knew my wife was dead. The whole sky to the south-west was black, and the wind blew out from under it in gusts of steadily increasing violence. It would be blowing us off the beach long before nightfall, and almost certainly raining as well. My whole mind steadily counted time on its way to half past five. I reckoned I could reasonably leave the house at five. Things would be terrible by then, and to go out walking at all would look like simple lunacy. But of course I no longer had to account to anyone for my actions. It was not always easy to remember that. Only I hoped tea would come on early, to give me time to get away without obviously rushing it.

The whole of that interminable afternoon I prowled about the dark shuddering house. As I had expected, the rain came down about half past three, driven against the southern and western windows with such violence that I thought at times it must be hail. The thing I remember most clearly, looking back, was coming upstairs and seeing Stella, in silhouette, looking out of a landing window at the black, tormented sea. She did not seem to hear me in the general uproar, but as I came up to her, she shivered suddenly and violently, and then turned and darted into the door of what had been Elizabeth's room. So far as I know, she never knew I was there. I did not see what she was doing in the empty bedroom. The door shut quietly behind her and I did not open it.

At four or soon after, just when I was getting worried about tea, she knocked on the door of my room and said, 'Jake? Tea.' It must have been quite unusually early, but I was too much relieved to notice this. It was already getting dark, even outside. The rain had lessened slightly, but it was blowing harder all the time.

We had the lights on for tea, which made it look darker than ever outside. We did not say much. Stella still seemed to be living in a different world, and I could think clearly of nothing but meeting Carol in an hour's time out on that storm-lashed beach. I was beginning to worry now that the weather might make it impossible for her to come and to wonder what I should do if she did not. We finished tea and Stella took the things out soon after half past four. From then on I was obsessed with the actual physical details of my going out. I do not think I ever looked beyond my projected meeting with Carol. I certainly had not made any coherent plans what to do in the light of its various possible outcomes. I was aware only of a desperate urge to get to her, that overlay, but only partially obscured, an inexplicit but almost bottomless apprehension. With the top of my mind I worried about what to wear on my head and feet. The time moved on towards five o'clock and the chaos outside turned steadily to dusk.

At ten to five I went upstairs to my room. I took off my jacket and put on another sweater. I wound a cotton scarf round my neck and tucked the ends into the neck of the sweater. My cap, mackintosh and gumboots were all together in the hall downstairs. It could not possibly take me more than thirty seconds to put them on. I walked to the window and looked out across the top of the wood. I had no lights on, and found that it was less dark outside than I had supposed. The whole ridged expanse of dark green leaves was rolling in waves under the force of the gusts. I had never seen the wood so much at the mercy of the wind. I was glad of this, because it seemed to lessen the power of the wood itself, which I had become increasingly aware of.

I went out of the room, shutting the door carefully behind me. I went downstairs to where the coats were hanging. I took off my shoes and put on the gumboots. I belted the heavy mackintosh round me, took down my cap and made for the front door. The kitchen door opened and Stella put her head out. I started looking for words, but she did not say anything. For a second or two we looked at each other in the dark hall. Her face was quite expressionless, but she was very pale. Then she drew back into the kitchen and shut the door. I jammed my cap down on my head, opened the door and stepped outside.

The door faced east, and for a moment I was aware of nothing but noise. There was a high pitched and almost continuous roar, in which the voices of wind and sea combined. Then as I went down the path, a gust came round the corner of the house and almost threw me at the gate. I turned right and made for the beach, head down into the wind.

CHAPTER NINETEEN

The tide must have been full high and had the whole force of the wind behind it. The seas were hitting the beach at its steepest part. They came in, as always, aslant, and were sucked back under the next crest in a continuous sideways slicing movement that was horrible even to watch. I saw white stones the size of a man's head galloping sideways down the slope in the grip of the sluicing grey water. A man who walked into that would be clubbed insensible and broken up before he had time to drown. I turned my back on the wind and sea and made my way up towards the top of the beach. The dark trees hung on grimly to the last of the land and roared together in the grip of the wind. I should not have minded going into the wood now. It was a fellow sufferer stronger than I was, and I could have taken some comfort from it. But my place was at the top of the beach. I walked up and down there, alternately throwing my weight back to resist the driving pressure of the wind behind me and forcing my way, almost crouching, into it. The sensible thing would have been to stand still, but I could not do that.

I do not know how long it was before I saw Carol coming towards me. I had forgotten that she would have to come all along the beach from the bottom of the tarmac road. She seemed to come unbelievably slowly. She looked so small in that grey chaos and moved so slowly into the wind, that I had the illusion that she was much farther away than in fact she was. It was like watching a figure through a telescope moving almost imperceptibly through a vast landscape. Then quite suddenly she came into focus again, and was only a short distance from me. I ran to her across the pebbles, clumsily, with the wind driving me. We met and clung together, I with my legs spread and my weight back against the wind, she leaning against me for shelter. She was as breathless as if she had climbed a cliff to get to me. It was a good deal darker now. The nearest trees crouched and roared barely ten yards above me.

For perhaps a minute she clung to me while she got her breath back, and during the whole time I believed that nothing was going to separate us. Then quite suddenly her hands tightened on my arms and she pushed herself back away from me and looked into my face. I knew at once then. I leant my head sideways to hear what she was saying, but I knew what it was going to be.

She said, 'Jake, he didn't kill your wife. You know that, don't you?'

'I don't know it. But I admit I can't prove he did. But Carol—'

'Jake, I can't get away. It's no good. I can't leave him. I don't want to try to explain. But it's no good, Jake.'

I knew it was irrelevant, but I said, 'But Carol, you love me, don't you?'

She pulled back away from me until she was hardly within arm's length. For quite a long time she looked at me. There, in that roaring chaos and near darkness, she looked at me steadily and almost dispassionately. Then she nodded, slowly and emphatically. 'Oh yes,' she said, 'I love you very much indeed. I have never loved anyone else and never shall.'

I suppose it was the nod that did it. No one who was not within a matter of feet could have heard anything she said. The first shot was fired as she stopped speaking. The charge ripped through the threshing leaves and whined, audibly even in that wind, just over our heads. I knew it was a twelve-bore and I knew that whoever it was still had the choke barrel in hand. In fact I think the second barrel was fired as I formulated the thought. I was too far from Carol to move her physically, but I had started to duck myself, willing her to do the same. I suppose to duck is common instinct. At any rate she ducked when I did, and the second charge went just over her head. One slug ripped through the dark hair and the silk scarf she had tied over it. It must have broken the skin. A small trickle of blood ran down her forehead, but she hardly seemed to feel it.

I caught hold of her and swung her down on to the pebbles. I felt the top of her head and found she was only scratched. Then I turned and ran towards the wood. This was not particularly gallant, but was in fact the only sensible thing to do. Whoever it was had to reload and might be put off by a frontal attack. In any case it was no good staying on the beach to be shot at out of cover, and he was not likely to try another shot at Carol with me pounding through the trees looking for him. I flung myself at the fence and went over it as I now knew how to. I did it very quickly at the cost of a long strip torn from my mackintosh. It was much darker in the wood, but also, surprisingly and immediately, a lot less noisy. The roar of the wind in the tops of the trees was continuous, but quite different in quality from the trampling of a running body through the undergrowth. I could hear someone running all right, but could not be sure where they were.

I turned eastwards instinctively. I suppose I assumed that that was where the attack had come from. It never occurred to me to think that I might be in danger. I was full of a blinding rage and wanted only to run after whoever it was until I caught them. I certainly had no clear idea what I should do when I did. I stumbled and swore in the semi-darkness, and the thicket slashed my face and hands and caught at my feet. The wood was full of a tangle of slight things that moved all the time and solid things that stood still. I was looking for a solid thing that moved. I never saw it, but presently I ran into a clearing and came face to face with a solid piece of darkness. It seemed grotesquely tall and quite motionless, but it had no branches. Dennis Wainwright had the gun pointing so directly at me that I almost blundered on to the muzzle before I saw what it was. When I saw, I stopped short, and he began to talk to me at once across the few feet of half-darkness that remained between us.

He said, 'I heard the shots too, Mr Haddon. Has anyone been hurt?'

I said, 'You ought to know, God damn it. Your wife is hit.'

'Carol hit?' He was full of a sort of angry concern, but no ordinary affection. It was like a man whose house has been robbed or a collector who has lost one of his most prized pieces. But the concern was intense and, now I come to think of it, unmistakably genuine, only I was too angry myself to let myself recognise its genuineness.

'Only a scratch,' I said. 'You went over her head. But only just. A couple of inches lower would have killed her.'

'I?' He suddenly screamed with rage. It was a womanish sort of noise to come out of that huge black figure in the middle of the dark wood. I was chilled at the pit of my stomach by the horror of his distress and by the first creeping suspicion that it was not, after all, Dennis Wainwright who had shot at us. He moved suddenly and there was a sharp click. He had broken the gun and thrust it at me. The two unfired cartridges fell into the mud behind him, but neither of us bothered with them.

'Look, Mr Haddon,' he said. He had stopped screaming, but his voice was hoarse and trembling. 'Look. Go on. See for yourself.'

I tilted the barrels up to the last of the daylight and squinted through them. There is no mistaking a dead clean barrel. The gun had not been fired. I handed it back and stood there gaping at him. He said, 'I have no wish to kill my wife, Mr Haddon. I do not want her dead. On the contrary, I cannot do without her at all. If anyone tried to take her away from me, I might well be tempted to consider murder, but it would not be her death I had in mind. She says you have been making love to her. I do not find that it makes very much difference to me what has happened. But you mustn't try to take her away from me, Mr Haddon. Do you understand? You must not try that at all. Perhaps you will believe that I did not want your wife killed either. It makes sense, doesn't it? I did not kill her. So far as I am concerned, her death was an accident I did not welcome. If you think somebody did kill her, you had better start looking at your end of the wood, don't you think? They will have reloaded by now, I expect, so you had better go more carefully than you came this way. Now I am going to take my wife home.'

He stooped and groped for the ejected cartridges. He wiped them very carefully and dropped them into his pocket. Then he tucked the gun under his arm and set off towards his end of the wood. I never saw him again. I turned and made up towards the central path. When I got to it, I ran westwards as fast as I could. Compared with the pace now possible in the wood, it was very fast indeed, but it was a blundering sort of run. A large part of my mind was concentrated on keeping on my feet and keeping moving. What with this and the bedlam going on above me, I was not thinking very clearly, but I knew I had to get back to the western end of the wood, and perhaps even the Holt House, as quickly as possible.

I did in fact fall once, but did myself no harm. Gumboots are very difficult to run in, but they will support a suddenly stretched ankle. I got to my feet and blundered on again. It was more or less completely dark in the wood now, and I was watching with an almost tearful desperation for a glimmer of daylight at the end of the path. There was in fact so little, even outside, that I felt the wind and heard the noise of the sea coming to meet me before I saw anything. When I did see a bit of sky, I saw simultaneously, against it, the dark outline of someone walking ahead of me along the path. I say 'walking' deliberately, because I had the clearest possible impression that this was so. The figure was straight up and almost stationary. Whoever it was might in fact have been standing in the path, but I think they were walking quite slowly. Then I stumbled and lost sight of them again. A moment later I almost ran into the stile.

I leant over it with the wind screaming in my face and looked across the open ground between me and the Holt House gate. There was no one there. Any sound I made as I ran up the path would have been blown back hard over my shoulder, but I suppose my last stumble might have been audible to anyone just ahead of me. With a thing like that the earth carries a lot of the sound. At any rate, whoever it was must have turned and melted into the trees a moment before I came to the stile. I turned my back on the wind and went a few paces back along the path. Then I turned and started to move southwards towards the beach. I went much more cautiously now. As Dennis Wainwright had pointed out, they would have had time to reload. But they were in the wood somewhere. Unless they were as clever at climbing the fence as I was, or could double back to the stile, I was going to come up with them some time. They could not be far.

After a bit I stopped, took off my mackintosh and rolled it into a tight ball big enough to shield my face and head. I did not know what sized shot they were using, but I reckoned that except at point blank range I could probably survive at least one barrel provided my head was safe. I was not sure a tightly rolled mackintosh would do the trick, but I thought it might at least help. I went forward steadily, peering over the top of my shield into the threshing darkness.

Now I come to think of it, it was a lunatic performance. On one assumption at least I was asking for trouble. On another I was at least not likely to be doing much good. On any assumption probably the best thing I could have done was to go back to the Holt House and do a little straight thinking. I suppose I kept on walking into the wood because I wanted above everything to avoid thinking straight. The urge to violent action was very strong, but I did not know what drove me or where it was driving me, and I dreaded being told.

At the bottom of the wood there was a sort of nightmare repetition of what had just happened at its western end. The wind and the bellowing of the sea came suddenly to meet me, and a much more luminous air that blew in across the white chaos of the breaking sea. I saw the fence in outline against it and, almost in front of me but a little to my right, a figure spread-eagled on it as though it was starting to climb. The figure was swathed and indeterminate, but I saw the long shape of the gun in its left hand. Once more, I do not know whether I gave myself away or whether the climb was abandoned as impracticable. I only know that one moment the figure was there stretched upon the fence and the next it had collapsed into a shapeless shadow and melted back into the trees. Unless I was very much mistaken, whoever it was had turned back to make for the stile.

I turned round myself and for the first and last time fell fairly heavily. It took me a little time to get myself up and find my bundled mackintosh, which I had flung away into the thicket as I fell. Then I started northwards again. I went faster and less cautiously now. The enemy either did not know I was there or was trying to get away from me. I did not think I was likely to be shot at. I made good progress, and believed I might now be ahead in the race for the stile. Whether it was a conscious race I still did not know. As I got near the path, I went more cautiously. I did not think that anything short of a yell or heavy fall was likely to be heard in the tumult except at very close range, but I wanted if possible to get to the stile undetected. I came out on to the path and stopped. I could just see the end of it from where I stood. The uproar was even greater here, as it always was close to the western edge of the wood. I could hear nothing like human movement, and did not really hope to.

I started to walk towards the stile, but as I got closer to it, it began to melt into the dark background of the open ground behind. I found that if I stooped, I brought the top bar at least against the sky. The sky was dark enough, but I did not think anything could move against it without my seeing it. In the end I actually dropped on to my hands and knees and crawled. It was like playing bears, but it did not occur to me to think it funny. Keeping the top bar of the stile always just in view against the sky, I crawled with an elaborate and cat-like precaution to meet whatever was coming up to it out of the trees. I got to within perhaps five yards of it and then stopped. I did not get up. I crouched there in the soaking mush and the raging darkness, never taking my eyes off the top bar of the stile.

The curious thing is that at the end of it all I heard it before I saw it. There was a faint but unmistakable iron-shod clatter. It was so like the noise my alpenstock had made on the stile that I knew at once what it was. A split second later something heaved into sight at the top of the stile and was gone again. I was up at once and running for the stile. The violence of the wind startled me as I hurled myself over it. Away ahead of me a dark figure, indeterminate but visible, was running over the open ground, prancing a little as it ran. It ran left-handed, making down towards the beach.

CHAPTER TWENTY

I was never sure at what point it became a conscious flight and pursuit. I am fairly certain it was not at first. I followed the prancing figure with its brandished weapon close enough to keep it just in view. Even this, running into the wind's eye, was as much as I could manage. I did not try to shout. Any sound I made might have been heard some way behind me but not a yard in front. Also, on the one occasion when I took breath to shout I did not like what I was going to say. In any case it could not go on. Neither of us had the legs of the other, and we could neither of us run indefinitely into that wind.

We came out on to the beach. There seemed to be light everywhere all of a sudden. The dark rim of land lay flat on our right, but the boiling sea was wholly white on our left and between them the endless avenue of wet grey pebbles threw back whatever light there was. Whenever it had happened, we were now conscious pursuer and pursued. At very much the same time I became aware of an almost desperate wish to call off the chase and go back to the house and also, mixed with it, a sick fear of what might happen if I did. I ran on, in two minds and in growing physical distress, until quite suddenly the chase was over.

We had followed a sloping line, edging down towards the breakers. I do not know how far we had gone westwards along the beach. Now, at a point perhaps twenty yards above the highest wash of the sea, the figure in front suddenly stood and slewed round, leaning back into the wind and pointing the gun straight at me. I dropped to a walk. I was desperately short of breath and, now I had stopped running, almost sick with physical fatigue. I walked slowly until I was not more than five yards from the muzzle of the gun. Then I stopped. 'Stella,' I said, 'Stella, for God's sake put that thing down and come back to the house.' I still had little breath and I had not allowed for the wind against me, even at that distance. I do not think she heard a word I said. She must have seen me speaking. We could see each other in some detail now. When she spoke, her voice had the wind behind it and came to me quite clearly, but in fits and starts, as the wind took hold of it or let it drop. She said, 'Is she dead? Is Mrs Wainwright dead?'

I shook my head and shouted at her into the wind. 'No. She's not hurt. Only a scratch.'

She nodded a little hopelessly. 'What a bloody mess,' she said. 'What a bloody mess I have made of it, haven't I?'

I took a step towards her and she immediately turned the gun away from me and on to herself. She had opened her mackintosh, so that the skirts blew straight out towards me, one on each side of her. She had a jersey and trousers under it. She put the muzzle of the gun hard against herself under her left breast. She held the stock with both hands, keeping one finger on the trigger. She said, 'Keep away, Jake, please. Don't come any closer. You've had enough blood on your hands, haven't you?'

I said, 'Where did you get the gun?' I really did want to know, and I had an instinct, which I still think was sound, to keep some sort of conversation going, even in that howling desolation and the state we were both in.

'I took it from Mike's. I think he must know I've got it, but he didn't see me take it. You know who I mean? Mike Grainger, at Seele.'

'Yes, I know. He came looking for it, I think.'

'Mike did? I never saw him.'

'No. I did. He asked me not to tell you.'

She half smiled. 'Good old Mike. He's a cheap skate really, but I suppose he has the elements of decency. Did you talk to him?'

'Yes. Then I went and saw him again and asked him questions. He told me about you – about you and him, I mean. Stella, was it really so essential that I shouldn't know?'

This time she really smiled, but the smile was a very watchful one. She said, 'Dear Jake, you're a fool, aren't you, in some ways? I can't think why I love you so much. Probably if Elizabeth hadn't got hold of you I shouldn't have. But there it was. Right from the start, as soon as she brought you home. I hope you'll never have to hate anyone as much as I hated her. It's a painful business.'

'But she's dead now.'

'Of course she's dead. I killed her. And now there's Mrs Wainwright. It's such a mess, don't you see? All these years, and then when she finally drove me to it, I found I was just a month too late. You'd got somebody else. If I'd known about that earlier, I think I might even have left her alone and watched her lose you. That would have been something, anyhow. But even that I got wrong. She said she wouldn't have me in the house any more, and I couldn't bear it and killed her. And then I found she had lost you anyway, and I had too, and I might just as well have left her alone. It's a mess, and there's no way out of it now.'

I said, 'But she couldn't—Oh well, it doesn't matter now. But it wasn't for Elizabeth to order you out of the house, was it? I could have insisted on your coming if you wanted to.'

'You insist? No, Jake dear. But it wasn't that. There was this thing with the Grainger man. Elizabeth got to know about it. God knows how, but I suppose it was easy enough. She probably gossiped locally. But I couldn't bear you to know about it. It wasn't very noble. Just casual lechery. Mike's pretty awful as a person, but he's so goddamned beautiful and I wanted something very badly. So that was it. I'd loved you nearly seven years, and there I was in bed with this small-time Romeo. And Elizabeth said if I came again, she'd tell you all about it. That was her mistake, the silly bitch. I couldn't have that and I couldn't bear not to come here, so there was no way out of it. I didn't plan anything, of course, but I knew if occasion offered I'd kill her. And things played right into my hands. They did, didn't they? I killed her and got clear away with it. I came down that evening just in time to see her trailing into the wood with all her stuff. I went into the house to find you, but you weren't there, and the car was gone. There was no one anywhere. I didn't think any more about it. I just walked straight across to the wood and killed her. I followed her. She made enough noise. I came up with her when she was fixing her things. She said you were in London and wouldn't be back till late, so it was a good chance for me to get all my stuff out of the house and go for good. And I'd better be gone before you came back. Then she turned her back on me and went on fiddling with her things. She was smiling to herself, as pleased as Punch. I didn't say anything. I just walked about looking for something to kill her with. I wanted a suitable stick, but it's odd when it comes to the point how difficult it is to find anything that will do. But I found one in the end. A nice solid branch, straight and heavy. I broke the twigs off it quite deliberately and tried it for balance. Then I walked back to where she was. She couldn't have heard me coming, because she had the headphones on. Not that I think she'd have worried. She was kneeling, leaning slightly forward. It was all grotesquely simple. She even took the headphones off just when I was wondering whether they mattered. I took a full swing and slugged her at the back of the neck, high up. She fell straight forward on her face and that was that. But of course I didn't know about the pigs. That was a bit crude but incredibly convenient. But in case you're worried, I think she was dead before they found her. They just covered in for me. They did it very well, I must say. It was bad luck on Dennis. It must have been the last thing he wanted. But he's an odd monster anyway. She won't be any good to you, you know, Jake – not after him. Anyway, I just drove back and took the Seele road. Nobody saw me. I spent the night at Seele. I told Mike I had come straight from London. I came on here next morning. I shouldn't have come as early as I did, but Mike's up at dawn, and I wanted to get to you at once. It worked, anyway. It was all perfect. And then I realised I was too late, and you'd taken up with the little Wainwright. I've taken some knocks in my time, but that beat everything. I thought for a bit nothing might come of it. I still don't think it's any use to you, but God knows I'm prejudiced. Anyway, I borrowed Mike's gun in case. And at the end of it all I missed her. Oh well. It doesn't matter now in any case. It's a very special gun, Jake. Mike's very fond of it, and I feel responsible. I should hate it to be damaged.' She took a quick pace towards me and swung the gun straight up into the air between us.

I have a passionate regard for guns, and Stella knew I had. I do not think anything in the world could have prevented me from trying to catch the gun rather than let it fall on the stones. It was very difficult to catch in the darkness and that wind, but I got a hand to it as it fell and held it. By that time she had ten yards start of me. She ran left-handed, along the beach, but always edging closer to the sea. She must have got her arms out of her mackintosh as she ran, because suddenly she flung it off and I found it a moment later encumbering my feet. When I got rid of it and went after her again, I could no longer see her. I ran on aimlessly, peering up and down the beach in the luminous darkness. Then I knew I had gone too far, and ran back. I was sobbing, but could not hear any sound I made. In the end I simply stood on the top of the sea-bank, leaning against the wind and looking down at the murderous chaos of white water and the endless flux of stones scuttering about under it. I never expected to see anything, but I went on looking until I found I was shivering helplessly with cold and physical exhaustion.

I broke the gun, but I think I already knew what I should find in it. It ejected two empty cases. She had never had more than the two rounds. Everything after that was bluff, and I had let her get away with it. The wind started me walking back. It simply blew me eastwards as my legs lost the strength to resist it. I stumbled in front of it along the beach, with the empty gun in my hands, full of a growing consciousness of total and intolerable loss.

Made in the USA
Lexington, KY
09 March 2013